SALINGER'S LETTERS

Nils Schou

SANDSTONEPRESS
HIGHLAND | SCOTLAND

First published in Great Britain and the
United States of America
Sandstone Press Ltd
Dochcarty Road
Dingwall
Ross-shire
IV15 9UG
Scotland.

www.sandstonepress.com

The publisher acknowledges support from Creative Scotland
towards publication of this volume.

ISBN: 978-1-910124-65-9
ISBNe: 978-1-910124-66-6

Cover design by Mark Ecob
Typeset by Iolaire Typesetting, Newtonmore.
Printed and bound by Totem, Poland

Nils Schou is a television writer and novelist based in his native Denmark. Born in Copenhagen in 1942 he is the author of many books. He really did correspond with Salinger and this is the originating point for his funny and wise novel, *Salinger's Letters*.

To Timme, William and Lillus

ONE

The Quest Begins

The call came at 9 p.m. It was April 17th, 1987.

A man's voice speaking with an American accent asked if I was Mr. Moller, Mr. Dan Moller.

I replied that I was.

'My name's Goldman, Arthur Goldman from New York,' he said. His voice was slightly nasal, low pitched.

He said he was a lawyer and mentioned the name of a firm consisting of a long list of names. Goldman, his own name, was the last one on the list. He would be in Copenhagen in five days, he said, and he would be staying at the Hotel d'Angleterre at Kongens Nytorv Square. Would I do him the honour of meeting him at the hotel on the day of his arrival? I asked what it was all about.

Something that could be of great benefit to both of us, was his reply.

'What kind of something?' I asked.

He would prefer to discuss it with me when we met, he said.

I asked him if he was sure he had reached the right Dan Moller.

As a young man did I go to dental school and live

at Nordisk Kollegium in the Osterbro section of Copenhagen, he inquired.

I did, I replied.

Then you're the right Dan Moller, he said.

We fixed the time for our meeting and then he breathed into the receiver, 'I think you should be there, this could really be to your advantage', and hung up.

Although I had racked my brains trying to guess what this could be about, I still had no clue when at 10.30 on a Thursday morning I walked into the lobby of the Hotel d'Angleterre.

Before I had made it over to the reception desk a small man wearing a light coloured suit approached me and smilingly exclaimed, you must be Dan, the writer, Dan Moller.

I asked him how he could tell.

'The way you're dressed,' he said and laughed aloud.

Before I had time to wonder whether there was a dress code for writers the man was shaking my hand and clapping me heartily on the shoulder with the other hand. 'I'm really glad to meet you, Dan! Really glad!' he said.

As to why he should be so glad to meet me I still had no idea.

He looked very young, very energetic, very Jewish-American. He was in his early thirties at the most, with close-cropped curly black hair that had begun to grey at the temples. He radiated a vitality and exuberance that made me like him at once. Everything was 'wonderful, just great, fabulous'.

A blonde woman in a red dress appeared behind him. The man introduced her as his wife, Rose. She acted as his travelling companion and secretary, he informed me.

Rose shook my hand and assured me she was very glad to meet me, too. Would I care to join them in the restaurant for a late breakfast?

'That would make us both extremely happy,' she said.

So much good will combined with the prospect of a breakfast at the window looking out on Kongens Nytorv Square was an offer I couldn't refuse.

I took the seat by the window in the vague hope that someone I knew would pass by and see me there. Like that woman from the Tax Collector's Office I met with the day before who had asked if writing was a hobby. Or the artistic director at the Royal Theatre who would never buy my plays because she only wanted to produce young playwrights. Or one of the critics that had panned my latest novel. I would nod to them pleasantly and they would be wondering how the hell I could afford to have breakfast at the d'Angleterre.

Arthur Goldman, who asked me to call him Art or Artie, and his wife Rose, who was charming and beautiful, spoke of the flight from New York to Copenhagen and about Scandinavia where they had spent their honeymoon a few years ago.

It was an excellent breakfast. I relished having a waiter by my side refilling my coffee cup whenever it was empty; nor was it an everyday occurrence, a waiter asking me at regular intervals if everything was ok, if the food was to my liking and if there was anything else he could get me.

The conversation drifted pleasantly across the table. Art and Rose mentioned that their good friend from the Upper East Side, Woody Allen, had stayed at the hotel 10 years before when he and Mia Farrow and a number of their children had been on a tour of Scandinavia. Among the children was Soon, the adopted daughter, who later became Woody's girlfriend and wife.

Art and Rose described the house Woody and his young wife were renovating on 85th Street.

I nodded, enjoying every minute of the breakfast and the pleasant company. The misunderstanding that undoubtedly was at the root of the situation would have to hold until the truth came out, at which point the breakfast would necessarily draw to a natural close.

In a sense this was a perfectly normal situation for me. I had no idea what I was doing here, no idea who these people were, and all I could feel was myself, whom I wasn't too comfortable with.

I was on my fifth cup of coffee, served by a solicitous waiter, when Art changed the course of the conversation and without preamble started talking business.

'Dan, good buddy', he said, 'A number of years ago you entered into correspondence with a famous American author.'

At that moment, at that very second, I caught sight of my wife on the other side of the window. She was walking her bike on the sidewalk in front of the d'Angleterre, smiling sweetly at me, with a mocking look that clearly said, 'There goes a man with a huge bank overdraft bumming a cup of coffee.' She mounted her bike and rode off quickly down the sidewalk.

My first thought was, 'Oh no, they're going to give her a ticket for riding a bike illegally on the sidewalk. A ticket is just what we don't need given the current state of our finances.'

Art and his wife were taking some papers out of a briefcase. Rose pushed one of the papers over to me and said, 'To our knowledge you have received between 50 and 70 letters from J.D. Salinger over the years, maybe more.'

I was 45 years old. I had always told my children I would live to be 90. In other words I had reached the halfway mark. For the most part I groped around in the dark without much direction. I'd been doing that all my life though. I'd got used to it.

In a fraction of a second all the pieces fell into place. This was no mistake.

Yes, I had been in correspondence with J.D. Salinger since the late 1960s although I wasn't sure about the number of letters. J.D. Salinger, the world-famous author, the recluse who had never given a proper interview in his life except to a schoolgirl writing for a local school newspaper in Cornish, New Hampshire, had written back when I wrote to him for the first time.

His novel, *The Catcher in the Rye*, which was published in 1951, had won him international acclaim. But I hadn't written to him about that. I had written about something else and anyway his later work, particularly *Frannie and Zooey*, interested me more.

The reason he had answered me was without a doubt due to his interest in Soren Kierkegaard; he even quotes him in the foreword to one of his books.

We had kept up the correspondence for a number of years. Mostly the letters were about Kierkegaard. The tone of his letters was like the tone of his books, personal, friendly, and between the lines you could sense the underlying humor and a certain desperation.

I got the impression of a tormented man who often felt lonely. I suspected I had caught him at a time in his life when he was glad to hear from an admirer who not only lived at a safe distance, but who cycled daily through streets formerly trodden by Soren Kierkegaard.

Salinger wanted to know if any descendants of Kierkegaard's brothers and sisters were still alive. He also hoped I could do him a big favour. Was a certain book about Kierkegaard by one of Kierkegaard's contemporaries, a book containing every bit of contemporary gossip about him, to be found in any of the second-hand bookstores of Copenhagen? I found the book and Salinger thanked me profusely. I wondered how he could understand what was in it.

Salinger was a great writer, no doubt about it. But part of his fascination was the fact that he had rejected what all other writers lap up. He refused to make any kind of comment or statement; he refused to give interviews. As it turned out, the myth of the Greta Garbo of literature, the media-shy poet, had made him a legendary celebrity. I was fascinated by the myth myself.

Over the years I had collected all the bits and pieces of information about him that occasionally dribbled down the wall he had erected between himself and the rest of the world. I was sure no one else in Europe knew as much about Salinger as I did, at least not in Denmark.

'Are you still in possession of those letters?' asked Art and Rose in unison.

'Yes,' I replied without hesitation. At the back of my mind though, I was wondering where the letters could be after so much moving from one house to another. Were they stashed away in a box in the attic? I recalled the shared attic in the commune where we used to live in the 70s; whenever people moved out, whether in anger or because they had got divorced or fallen in love or for any other reason, they would freely help themselves. Were my letters from J.D. Salinger languishing in a cardboard box somewhere, yellowed with age, in a damp basement of some unknown fellow commune dweller?

Hell with that, I thought, letters are supposed to be read when you get them. They're personal and the only person they should concern is the recipient.

At this point Art told me how much he was prepared to pay for the letters and I changed my mind.

Rose repeated the amount.

The two Americans stared at me fixedly. I must have looked as if I had gone into shock because Rose wrote down the amount in large figures on a napkin and pushed the napkin towards me.

My initial reaction was that this was some kind of sick joke. Somebody wanted to make fun of me, humiliate me. Or maybe this was some kind of Candid Camera stunt and hidden photographers were filming my facial expression. 'Hungry author offered bone.'

I stared at the amount jotted on the napkin and kept on staring until my eyelids got so heavy I thought I was going to lose consciousness or simply fall asleep and continue dreaming sweet dreams.

Rose and Art Goldman repeated the amount. When I still didn't react Rose pointed to the napkin where the amount was written.

This was unnecessary; I had understood it first time round.

I had no idea what to say.

Art and Rose looked as though they were prepared for this. They explained they were acting on behalf of an anonymous buyer. The market for letters written by celebrities had exploded in recent years. At the top of the list of letters by literary figures was J.D. Salinger. Number two was Hitler, which surprised me until Art explained that Hitler appeared in several categories including as the author of 'Mein Kampf'. This information made me feel better. Salinger would enjoy hearing he had beaten the author, Adolf Hitler, when it came to the value of celebrity letters.

I tried to collect my thoughts. Unfortunately they tend

to run off in all directions, which is how I earn my living. That's how all writers earn their living so I wouldn't want to change it.

I needed to talk to my wife.

Apart from decisions such as what to have for dinner I talk all decisions over with my wife.

I promised Art and Rose I would get in touch with them as soon as I had consulted my wife.

I biked around town trying to locate her. As far as I could remember she had a workout class and a hair-dresser's appointment before going to work. She's a dentist and works on the third floor in a building on the corner of Borgergade and Gothersgade. She was in the middle of a root canal treatment when I burst in.

One of the things she finds most irritating about me is that when I want to talk to her it has to be *now*. She thinks that must be one of the reasons I chose my profession. Writers by definition have to be childish, otherwise they couldn't be writers.

When I told her what had happened though, she pushed her irritation aside. What should I do? I demanded.

'Nothing,' she replied. 'Absolutely nothing. If they're interested now they'll be interested tomorrow and in a month from now.'

She went back to her patient and her root canal treatment.

I followed her advice. I biked back to Kongens Nytorv Square and met with Rose and Art at the d'Angleterre. I needed more time to think things over, I said.

They were courtesy itself. They had apparently been prepared for my reaction. What if they invited my wife and me and any of our children who cared to come to New York for a little vacation, they suggested, all expenses paid. We could discuss the situation more thoroughly at our leisure. 'No obligations,' they emphasized. No matter what I decided regarding the letters the trip would be free.

'What does your wife say?' asked Rose.

'It's not so much what she says. It's more what she doesn't say,' I replied.

Rose nodded knowingly. 'That's what most marriages are like, Dan'.

'Yes, I'm beginning to think so too.'

'What about taking her on a little trip?' Rose suggested.

Art Goldman took an envelope out of his jacket pocket and waved it in front of me.

'Dan, here's a tailor-made credit card just for you issued to my law firm. Buy any kind of plane ticket you like and stay at any hotel you want in New York.'

I opened the envelope. At the top of the credit card stood my name. The card looked as if it was made of pure gold. In the glow of the golden card my thoughts exploded in all directions. I had a vision of myself showing the gold card to my wife and daughters. They couldn't believe it. I saw us walking down the street to the ATM on the corner. Money would pour out of the ATM until we were swimming in it until finally I couldn't swim anymore, I would be drowning in money.

In short my brain was behaving like any normal writer's brain; it started working overtime.

When I had come to myself, standing there in the lobby of the d'Angleterre, I hastened to accept. Yes, please.

So that's what we did. I hoped I wouldn't suddenly wake up and realise the whole thing was just a daydream.

My wife accepted. She would find a substitute at the dental clinic. Our two daughters had just got new boyfriends and didn't want to go anywhere. My parents promised to look after them.

I knew which hotel to stay at, too: the Hotel Pioneer on the corner of Broome Street and the Bowery, the place where poor Danish writers stay these days when they're in New York.

Art and Rose assured me that staying somewhere more upmarket was no problem.

There was no reason to explain the feeling of sinfulness that keeps me from staying at anything but the lousiest hotels, preferably with cockroaches and where the plumbing doesn't work. A week in luxury at the Plaza would bring me to the brink of despair. I wanted to tell them that J.D. Salinger would *never* stay at the Plaza. It would be *phony*!

TWO

The Quest Continues

We stayed at the Pioneer the last week in April. Double room, no bath, no cockroaches. I had brought the bundle of letters with me, the cause of it all.

Our only luxury was a taxi from 42nd Street down to the hotel. The driver was from the Dominican Republic and the whole time he kept nodding his head to the beat of 'You Can't Hurry Love', sung by the Supremes. It was a song of the 60s and I had heard it the year I began writing to Salinger.

The letters were in a plastic folder and I hadn't let them out of my sight the whole trip across the Atlantic. They were our meal ticket, they were paying for our hotel, our meals, our Metro cards for the bus and the subway. At night I slept with them under my pillow. The letters were our justification for being in New York.

I was terrified someone would break into the Hotel Pioneer and steal the letters. The rumor they were worth a fortune would have preceded us to New York. I lay awake at night listening to the traffic noises down in the street. The door would be smashed in. Masked robbers armed with revolvers would burst into the room and order me to hand over the letters without a struggle, or else. 'Hand over the Salinger letters. Now, motherfucker!' My inveterate writer's brain was hard at work.

A trip to NY was an offer that I couldn't bring myself to refuse. However, that was as far as I could go. I was determined not to sell the letters.

This decision didn't make me feel I was conning Art. There was a poetic justice in the idea that my former correspondence with Salinger was paying for our stay in the city Salinger had lived in as a young man and where the action of his classic novel, *The Catcher in the Rye*, unfolds.

The rules of the game demanded that I meet with Arthur Goldman and his wife at a lawyer's office on 57th Street. My wife came too. I placed the letters on the table in front of the Goldman couple They pored over them, studying them carefully for a long time. A respectful silence reigned in the room.

When they had finished reading they asked if they could take a photocopy.

No, I said.

They then increased the amount of their original offer. This time they didn't say the amount aloud, they wrote it on a piece of paper which they pushed over the table to us. My wife read it and said, 'My God, Dan, that's your pension.'

'What are you talking about, pension? I'm young!'

'You're not young, you're just childish.'

'I'll be childish till I die.'

'Hey, listen, there are writers out there who aren't childish.'

'Who? Name me one. Just one!'

'Dan, calm down. Take it easy.'

'I'm not selling those letters.'

'For Chrissake. You're acting like the hero of one of your own sentimental stories.'

'I'm not selling'

'So don't sell, Asshole!'

We were speaking Danish so we could talk freely. We tried to make our voices sound as neutral as possible. I kept my hands under the table so Rose and Art couldn't see how much they were shaking.

'Who's the buyer?' I asked Art.

Unfortunately, he said, he was bound by client confidentiality not to reveal his client's identity.

'Is it Salinger?' I asked.

Art's face was expressionless. 'Let's just say it's someone who feels close to Salinger.'

'Have you met Salinger?' I asked.

Art hesitated. 'I'm in correspondence with him.'

'Can you call him now?'

Art smiled broadly as though he was enjoying this game of ping-pong.

'Possibly,' he said.

Now my hands and feet both were shaking under the table. I girded my loins and came out with the phrases I had rehearsed so carefully.

I said, 'If the party who wishes to purchase the letters

is either Salinger himself or a member of his immediate family, he can have them for free. On one condition.'

Art didn't look at all surprised. 'What's the condition?'

'That I get to meet Salinger and get to have the first ever interview with him.'

Art was an experienced negotiator. He didn't bat an eye. His hands on the table in front of him were absolutely still. He fixed me with an unwavering gaze for a long time.

The seconds crawled by and became minutes without his saying a word. His eyes still fixed on me, he made a sign with the index finger of his left hand to Rose, who was sitting next to him. Rose took a diminutive cell phone out of her jacket pocket. She entered a number and handed the phone to Art.

Art waited 20 seconds before the phone was answered.

'Mr. Salinger?' said Art in his low-key, nasal New York voice. 'Art Goldman in New York. I'm sitting here with your Danish friend and his lovely wife. Here's the deal they propose. You get the letters free and he gets to meet you and get an interview.'

Art listened to what was said on the other end. It was a short message. Then he stood up, held out his hand and said, 'You'll hear from us by evening. Mr. Salinger wants to think over the offer.'

When we were down on 57th Street again my wife exploded. 'Why the hell don't you just sell him the damned letters so we can have some money for once?'

'It's a long story,' I said. 'But all my life I've dreamed of meeting the man, just once.'

15

'Can't you just meet him, give him the letters and dash over to the bank with the money. We need a new kitchen and a new bathroom and a new floor in the living room.'

'I know. Let me think. I'm kind of confused right now.'

'You're *always* confused and you *never* think!'

'You know that isn't true. I'm always thinking, just not the way you think.'

'Listen Dan, don't give me that bit about how I'm that boring little dentist who somehow or other just happens to pay all the bills.'

'You knew perfectly well what you were getting yourself into.'

'That excuse wore pretty thin a long time ago.'

The telephone in our room rang the same evening.

'It's Art', said the low, self-contained voice. 'You'll be picked up outside your hotel tomorrow morning at 9 a.m. Mr. Salinger will be waiting in Cornish, New Hampshire. He will give you the first and last interview of his life. In return you will give him the letters.'

I couldn't sleep all night, naturally. The idea appealed to me. When my wife had fallen asleep I left the hotel and wandered the streets of New York until the sun came up. I walked and walked. I was troubled. Being troubled is good for me. I was upset. That's good too, and so is being uneasy, nervous and confused. I didn't want to miss one second of what was going on in the city around me or what was happening inside me.

As a writer my sole material is what's happening inside me. I keep track of every single thought. Actually I would rather have been a dentist. That's what I was trained for and that's what I did until a woman I had never seen before came into my life. Without that woman I would still be a dentist. But instead I found myself committed to a childish, self-absorbed and somewhat ridiculous line of work. I was a writer, a writer without the least bit of imagination. I don't invent anything. The material comes to me. I am merely the attentive observer. What's going on? What's passing through my mind? That's what I was eager to discover as I walked the streets of New York that night in April, 1987.

Of course what came to me was what was bound to come. As Tove Ditlevsen said, 'You open the closet and your childhood comes tumbling out.'

My youth, my childhood and my entire life basically consist of just one thing: depression. Out of the closet tumbled depression.

If I didn't suffer from depression we wouldn't be in New York now.

Depression was the reason why Salinger and I had been in correspondence for all those years. His depression and mine.

The streets of New York that night in April were the perfect setting for letting my thoughts drift back in time, back to all the people that had led to Salinger and our trip to New York.

THREE

Back Into the Shadows

I have depressive personality disorder. I've had it all my life.

I was quite young when I learned I had to hide my depression; no one wants to hang out with someone with depression. Depression is contagious. One of the first things I mastered when I was at school was how you're supposed to look when you're happy.

Another thing I understood at an early age was that there's not just one kind of depression; no two depressions are alike. Depressions keep changing, they develop. You have to find out for yourself what your depression consists of, what it looks like. You scrutinize yourself, well aware you could be wrong. You examine your own reactions, you're your own doctor. It's unremitting, hard work and in all probability doomed to failure; most people give up in advance.

Some people compare having depression to having cancer. They wish there was some kind of chemotherapy for depression, and there is. Antidepressants are pretty much the only treatment for depression. In many cases the medication works and the patient and their families are duly grateful. But if they don't work you have to be your own doctor. You have to figure out for yourself what people, what places, what situations have an anti-depressant effect on you.

When I was a child I thought everybody was like me. Later I realised that most children are happy, full of a zest for life.

I wasn't just an unhappy child. I was depressed. I was suffering from an illness.

My parents tried to find someone who could cure me. They took me to specialists. A number of people tried to help. All kinds of approaches were tried: medication, electroshock therapy, talk therapy. It seemed I was resistant to all of them. Many of the people I met while we were undergoing treatment committed suicide. When I was fifteen I contemplated different methods of committing suicide. I carefully studied all the different ways you could take your own life. My choice fell on hanging. Two of my friends had hanged themselves, one from a chandelier hook in his room, the other out in the woods one night.

I discovered that for me the best antidepressant was to carefully observe my inner processes and write them down.

From the age of fifteen I've treated myself 24 hours a day. I kept it to myself, but the girls I fell for fled as soon as they realised. I wanted to tell them everything, but of course none of them wanted to listen.

I was a compulsive talker. When I was a child I talked so much that my parents and family would say, 'Would you please just shut up for a minute, Dan. You're driving me crazy talking all the time.'

I talked incessantly until I was six. I would say the first thing that came into my mind. Then from my first day at school it became an inner monologue in my head, not a word would escape my lips. From that day on I've talked continuously, unceasingly, but only as an interior monologue. I discovered other people don't do that. I yearned for the day when I would stop talking all the time.

I was filled with excessive longing for other people to like me. At the boy scout summer camp I went to, one of the boys was selected as Scout of the Year. I spent every second I was in that camp running back and forth in front of the scoutmaster busily performing chores. My deepest wish was to be recognised as the most popular boy scout of the summer. It never happened.

My friends could experience things without having to talk about it with other people. I couldn't enjoy it if I hadn't told someone. In High School I often heard a classmate say, 'He's just like a three-year-old who hurts his knee and doesn't cry until he's run home and told his mother.'

I dreamed of the day when I would be able to experience something without having to tell anyone.

I didn't know whether this was a symptom of depression, but I did know that it was what made me different from other people.

They had eyes to see with; I had no eyes. I always

saw everything through other people's eyes. I dreamed of having my own eyes one day.

Certain situations can have an antidepressant effect, certain people, objects, colours, sounds. Most of the time you don't know why.

I am, and have always been, a large-scale consumer of medication and pills. I'll try just about anything. I would visit people and go to the bathroom looking for the medicine chest. I would steal medication for arthritis, sleeping pills, painkillers, anti-epileptic drugs, stimulants, whatever. In my experience just about any pill has a mild antidepressant effect.

I've tried all the hard drugs; they all have an antidepressant effect.

Liquor is good for depression. So is rain, a good fight, coffee, cigarettes, and bad sex.

Just about anything can have an antidepressant effect, but only on a superficial level. The depression always returns when the drug wears off.

I've filled piles of yellowing notebooks with good advice over the years. I've collected advice from any number of sources. Useful advice can be found anywhere; user's guides are particularly helpful. In a paint store I found a booklet on anti-rat pest control, figuring that rats were comparable to depression. That booklet was one of the most effective introductions to depression I've ever encountered.

Nobody really knows what depression is or where it comes from. This is a fact that many people find difficult to accept. You have to write your own user's guide. It's hard, time-consuming work and will most likely end in failure and defeat.

During one period of my life when I was particularly depressed I tried rat poison as an antidepressant. Afterwards I thought it might have been an unconscious wish to commit suicide. But the fact was that rat poison proved to be one of the most effective antidepressants I had ever tried. For days I walked around in a mild daze, close to feeling something approaching happiness or joy. I daily increased my dose of rat poison until I ended up collapsing in the street and was rushed to the hospital to have my stomach pumped. That was my last experiment with rat poison.

Over the years I've been examined regularly to determine whether I'm autistic, schizophrenic, psychotic or paranoid. Every time the answer is the same: I just have ordinary, run-of-the-mill depression.

When I was a child one of my therapists was an old lady who lived in an apartment on Valby Langgade, Mrs. Magnussen. She suffered from depression herself and experimented with alternative treatments. We played music together. Music had proved to have an excellent effect on certain forms of depression. On me it had the opposite effect; music, especially beautiful classical music, made me even sadder.

Mrs. Magnussen tried to devise a therapy tailored to my case. She knew I was a compulsive talker without ever opening my mouth. She told me I should try letting the words come out. She didn't have to say it twice. I opened my mouth and let everything I was saying to myself pour out. She listened patiently to all the murders, mutilations, blood and destruction that gushed from my lips. I could have kept it up for hours, days, weeks. Mrs. Magnussen was the only therapist who had seemed to like me.

When I was in High School I was an in-patient at a psychiatric hospital on several occasions. They gave me antidepressants and talk therapy.

Since nothing seemed to help, my parents tried a number of alternative therapies. There was primal scream therapy. I was supposed to yell as loud as I could while beating a pillow that I was supposed to imagine was my mother and father. But I've always been very fond of my parents and even though I tried hard to mobilise the hidden anger I was supposed to feel against them, I never could.

There lived a woman in Birkerod who did fairytale therapy. Her name was Ulla Ladegaard, and I liked her from the start.

She looked as though she had just stepped out of a fairy tale herself. She didn't look like a witch, she looked like a princess. Even though she was old she dressed like a girl. She dyed her hair red and wore rings on all her fingers. Ulla Ladegaard taught me how to step into a fairy tale and seek out someone wicked to slay later on. This could also be an evil beast or an impersonal force. Anyone could do this exercise or therapy. We went through Grimm's fairy tales and Hans Christian Andersen's fairy tales and obscure Croatian, Italian and German fairy tales that Ulla had collected. I chopped the heads off trolls, off death, off the devil, off black dogs. They all symbolised my depression.

I really liked Ulla but no matter how many dragons I slew it didn't make my depression go away or even grow any less.

The last time I saw Ulla she had called in her sister, who was a fortune teller, a clairvoyant. She pored over my palm and then burst into tears.

Ulla apologised, but there was no need. You didn't need a fortune teller to know that things would not go well for me.

Ulla from Birkerod taught me how to give my depression faces. Faces, adventures, quests. Depression was not just an impersonal grey rot engulfing me; it had evil-looking avatars beckoning me into their universe.

I invented long tales in which I was lured into dark forests. Deep in the forest, in the dark, a huge hound would be lying in wait, or a troll or a lion. This creature was the depression. If I vanquished the monster either by force or by cunning the depression would disappear.

The tales filled my life when I was in High School. On the outside I was a normal student. No one suspected the orgies of violence and bloodshed raging within me. Not until I graduated from High School and started dental school did my depression stop having different faces; the faces merged into one face and only one face.

24

As soon as the face emerged I immediately called Ulla to thank her. Without her help, the face would never have come to light.

She laughed when I told her. 'Dan, you have no idea how happy that makes me. It was bound to happen.'

'Why was it bound to happen?'

'Because you try so hard. You expend more strength than you have. But remember, my dear, life is and will always be a quest. We're all of us a little lost out there in the dark woods, you're not the only one. We're all seeking the love that moves the sun and the stars.'

'What does that mean?'

'Oh, you'll find out some day. When you do, think of me, Dan.'

The road that led to all the different monstrous faces merging into just one face went past a professor at the School of Dentistry.

Professor Ib Schroder, Dr. Odont, was my teacher of pharmacology and corrective jaw surgery during my fourth year. He was an ugly little man with a pockmarked face that made him look like a frog. He had been tortured during the war and for many years had been an alcoholic and a manic depressive. When I met him he hadn't touched a drop for several years and was no longer manic depressive; he was only depressive. He knew I was depressive too because we had often been patients together in the psychiatric ward at Rigshospitalet. We had spent hours and days together in the corridor comparing notes on our depression.

As a pharmacologist at the School of Dentistry he had access to all kinds of drugs and pills. He had a friend, a fellow professor, who was experimenting with LSD as a treatment for depression. Schroder invited me to join them.

The session took place at his friend's apartment on Strandboulevarden, the same building Georg Brandes used to live in. There was a plaque on the wall commemorating it. By chance the building was only a stone's throw from Nordisk Kollegium, the residence hall I was living in.

On a Wednesday evening at the end of November 1966, six of us lay down on mats in the professor's living room. He gave us each a thin piece of paper on which he had placed a small dose of LSD. We were instructed to keep the paper under our tongue until it dissolved.

We each had a different reaction. Two had anxiety attacks, one remained lying down shaking with laughter, one felt sick and had to make a mad dash for the bathroom to vomit. In my case everything grew quiet and peaceful, with music and colours that seemed to last forever. I was greeted by schoolmates I hadn't seen for years. None of them said anything, they just waved at me and disappeared. I took the train to Birkerod in my imagination. Ulla Ladegaard was waiting for me at the station. This was something that had never happened in reality. We walked through the town to her house. We sang together, something we had never done either. We sang tunes by the Mamas and the Papas with homemade

Danish texts. The songs were about autumn, leaves falling from branches and bare trees against an autumn sky.

Ulla and I passed her house and went into the woods. In my LSD high the woods were just behind her house. In real life there was a school there and a ball field. In the LSD woods we met some of the fairy tale figures she and I had invented together and that I had slain with my sword, one by one. This time I was content to greet them as we went deeper and deeper into the woods and it grew darker and darker. We were deep in the woods when I realised that Ulla had fallen behind. I turned around and saw she was standing completely still.

'Ulla?' I called to her.

'Keep going, Dan', she said.

'Aren't you coming?'

'No, there's someone you have to meet and you have to go alone.'

I called to Ulla but she answered, 'I'm going home to die.'

'Die?' I cried and started towards her.

She stretched out both hands towards me and told me to stay where I was.

'My time has come Dan, and it's time you met the most important person in your life from now on.'

'Ulla! Come back! Stay here!' She had disappeared into the dark and I was alone. It was completely quiet in the woods. The only thing I could hear was my own breathing.

I heard footsteps somewhere but I couldn't see anything. The sound was being made by twigs snapping on the forest floor.

I could hear someone else breathing somewhere, someone humming. Was this someone I had met in one of my fairy tale adventures?

'Welcome, Dan', said a voice. 'Finally we meet.'

'Who are you?'

'You know who I am.'

'No.'

'I am someone you *have* to meet, someone you invented yourself.'

'A beast? A troll? Some creature I tried to slay?'

'No, you can never kill me.'

'Why not?'

There was the sound of laughter. 'Because if you kill me, you also kill yourself.'

'Is this some kind of guessing game?'

'I'm your own invention.'

'When did I invent you?'

'Just now.'

'Are you a man or a woman?'

'Can't you tell?'

'How old are you?'

'How old are *you*?'

'Are you my age?'

'Born the same year, the same month, the same week, the same time, the same place.'

'And I invented you myself?'

28

'You're inventing me as we speak, Dan Moller, student of dentistry.'

'Have you been following me?'

'Always, every day, all your life.'

There was a peal of thunder and a flash of lightning lit up the woods. Standing in a group of trees I saw a figure. It was a woman, a woman I didn't know, whom I had never seen before.

Lightning struck again twice and I got a good look at her.

She was slender with short hair and her eyes were hostile. She was dressed completely in black.

Another bolt of lightning lit up the woods.

She sneered, 'Bit melodramatic, don't you think, all that thunder and lightning?'

'Did you order it? Is it you that's being melodramatic?'

'Dear little Dan, you still don't seem to understand.'

'What don't I understand? That you're a monster in a fairy tale like all the others and I have to kill you now?'

'Do you want to commit suicide?'

'I don't want to, but I've thought about it a lot.'

She walked over to me and handed me a sword that she had been hiding behind her back. I took it. 'Where did you get that sword?' I asked.

'You gave it to me yourself. Now decide if you want to cut off my head or stab me in the heart.'

'Who are you?' I asked

'I'm Amanda.'

'Amanda?'

'Yes, that's the name you've given me.'

'When?'

'Now.'

'Amanda who?'

'Just Amanda.'

'What does Amanda mean?'

'It means 'She who shall be loved'.'

'Should I love you?'

'It's up to you. You created me.'

'Why should I love someone I don't know?'

'You know me. You know me as well as you know yourself.'

'How well do I know myself?'

She laughed. 'Only on a very superficial level. Like a stranger passing in the street.'

I felt I was being weighed down by a burden so heavy that I was brought to my knees on the forest floor.

Amanda quickly took two steps backwards.

'Stop being so pathetic, Dan. Kneeling down before me? That's really not my style.'

'You were the one that made me kneel,' I protested.

The pressure increased, forcing me down even further. I heard myself uttering words I hadn't actually thought of. 'Hey! I know who you are. You're Depression. You're my Depression.'

'With a capital D, I believe?'

'You're the depression in one of Ulla Ladegaard's fairy tales.'

'No, I'm the depression in one of Dan Thorvald Moller's fairy tales.'

'Welcome,' I said.

'Thank you.'

'What can you tell me about myself?'

'Only what you invent yourself, Dan.'

'Are you related to Ulla Ladegaard?'

'Ulla is dead, Dan.'

'Of course she's not dead. She took me into the woods to find you.'

I heard the sound of footsteps running over the twigs on the forest floor. Amanda was gone.

Amanda's disappearance coincided with my coming out of the acid trip. I was back in the apartment on Strandboulevarden in Osterbro.

My sense of time seemed to be out of whack. It felt like the trip had lasted for months. How long it had really lasted I didn't know.

On the way down the stairs Schroder wanted to know if the LSD had had any effect on my depression. I told him about Amanda.

It was dark and windy outside when we reached the street. I walked him to his bus stop on Claessensgade.

Four days later I read in the paper that Ulla was dead.

Four months later Schroder committed suicide by checking into a hotel on Vendersgade and emptying two bottles of pills. He left letters to his family, friends and colleagues. To my surprise he had also written me a letter even though I was only a student lab assistant in his department at the Faculty of Dentistry.

He told me he had been studying depression for many

years, his own and others'. If I was interested in reading his handwritten notes I should contact his daughter, Beate. He had left instructions as to where the notes were to be found, and had authorised her to let me read them. At the end of the letter he signed off: 'All the best, yours devotedly, Ib Schroder. P.S. Say hello to Amanda! Give her the attention and love she deserves. She's the way forward for you.'

The letter was in my mailbox at the ground floor entrance to Nordisk Kollegium on Strandboulevarden. I read it on the way up the stairs to my room, South Wing, nr 42.

The phrase 'yours devotedly' and especially the word 'devotedly' struck me with an almost physical force. No one had ever written 'yours devotedly' to me. It seemed a highly emotional way to close a letter. Later I found out it was how men of Schroder's generation usually signed off.

The fact that he asked me to say hello to Amanda didn't interest me much. After Amanda had entered my life as a permanent fixture, another woman had turned up who changed my life in ways I could never have imagined in my wildest dreams.

FOUR

The Feather Factory

Nordisk Kollegium residence hall was for male students only. It was sponsored by Nordisk Fjerfabrik. The feather factory itself was across the railroad tracks out by the harbour.

Living at Nordisk Kollegium was a scholarship; you had to get high scores on your initial exams to qualify. The residence hall consisted of two wings. The third wing housed the factory's administration building, with the dormitory's dining hall and student lounge on the ground floor. One of the provisions of the scholarship was that we were given two meals a day, served by women dressed in black with white aprons. Our beloved Mrs. Filt was in charge of the whole thing.

In the basement beneath the south wing was an indoor soccer facility. Every evening after dinner there were soccer tournaments. I was the regular defender on a team consisting of two dental students and three medical students. Not a talented soccer player, my only claim to fame was that I could keep going indefinitely. One Sunday I played 10 hours at a stretch. Soccer did not have an anti-depressive effect on me, but it did let me enter into my exhaustion and fatigue and come out the other side struggling into more fatigue and more exhaustion until on the verge of collapse.

I often kept going past the point of collapse and I would keel over on the playing field. Very few of my fellow players knew I suffered from depression.

One of those who did know was a medical student called Michael Bonnesen. He was doing a psychiatry internship at Rigshospitalet and had read my medical journal without knowing it was mine. We ran into each other in the hall.

I was sitting in the corridor nodding drowsily as I had been heavily sedated.

He sat down next to me. 'Hi, I didn't know you had depression.'

'Well, I do.'

'Couldn't tell by looking at you. You hide it really well.'

'Thanks.'

'I'll keep it to myself, of course.'

'Thanks, Michael.'

Michael Bonnesen was the natural centre of attention wherever he went. The residence hall was full of people studying history and literature, and Michael's friends seemed to have stepped right out of Danish history or Danish literature. He knew everyone worth knowing among the trendsetting, intellectual elite of the time: politicians, authors, resistance fighters, philosophers, university professors. He had sat on P.H.'s lap at the age of seven and smoked a cigar. He invited Mogens

Fog and Elias Bredsdorff to the lectures and debates he organised in the passageway between the student lounge and the dining hall. Klaus Rifbjerg and Villy Sorensen often came and gave readings. Michael was on first name terms with all of them.

Now he was sitting next to me in the corridor of the Psychiatric Ward at Rigshospitalet. He was an eager sportsman with a talent for any sport he touched. Beside me he looked like a vitamin commercial. As for me I just sat there with my shoulders hanging. I could barely keep my head up. I looked and felt like a decrepit old man.

We had never talked alone before. Our relationship was limited to playing soccer, but you get to know people on the soccer field too. Michael was the same friendly, energetic guy playing soccer as he was at meals, parties, and debates, always well-mannered and considerate.

He was no different the day we met in the hospital corridor. I didn't know whether his friendly interest was simply because he was being polite or because he was genuinely interested, but he had a way of asking questions that made me tell him everything he wanted to know about my depression. I was so heavily medicated I could hardly talk straight. Was it the medical student, the future neurologist questioning me, or was it my soccer buddy from the dorm? I didn't care, I'd talk to anyone willing to listen.

When I told him about Amanda he jumped up so suddenly he spilled coffee all over his pants.

'Amanda? Your depression is called *Amanda?*'

'Yes, what's wrong with that?'

'Is she always with you?'

'When the depression is there she's there.'

'And when the depression goes away?'

'Then she's not there. I don't know where she goes.'

'Do you talk to her?'

'I talk to her and she talks to me.'

'Is she there now?'

'And how!'

'Is she saying anything?'

'Just a second, let me listen.'

I listened to what Amanda was saying. 'She knows all about you and your family, Michael. She knows who your father is and your mother and your grandparents and your uncles.'

'Hey, Dan, wake up, buddy. Dan, can you hear me?'

'Of course. It's just that my eyelids are so heavy I can barely keep my eyes open.'

'Tell me something, Dan.'

'Sure.'

'You make it sound like Amanda knows something you don't know.'

'Right.'

'Can you ask her something for me?'

'Sure. I can ask her anything.'

'Ask her what she thinks of me,' said Michael.

I did what he asked. He fixed his gaze on me and I knew what he was looking for. He wanted to see if my lips were moving. They weren't.

Then I told him what Amanda thought of him.

'The key words for you are sympathy, affinity, affection. People like you. The opposite of sympathy is antipathy, aversion, dislike. Amanda is always going on about sympathy. She thinks about it a lot. I won't bore you with everything she says about sympathy. She says it's an endless concept, bottomless.'

Michael remained at my side until I fell asleep.

A few days later when I was back in the dorm he knocked on my door one evening and asked, 'How would you like to meet my sister?'

I gave him my usual cold response. 'Why should I want to meet your sister when I don't even *know* your sister?'

Such trifles didn't bother Michael. 'My sister doesn't want to meet you, she wants to meet Amanda.'

'Amanda?'

'Yes, Amanda.'

'Does your sister know Amanda?'

'Don't you remember? You told me about Amanda over at the hospital?'

'Sure I remember. '

'I'm having a party in the kitchen on Saturday. Can you come?'

'Sure. Thanks.'

'See you there then. Want to play some soccer?'

'Sure,' I said.

The first time I saw Puk Bonnesen, Michael's little sister, was when she walked into the kitchen passageway that Saturday night at 7 p.m. She looked like a parody of a well brought up, well-mannered High School girl even though she was 22. In the meantime I had gleaned some information about her from the lit students at the dorm.

She was a kind of prodigy. She had already written two collections of poems and a novel that was very likely autobiographical. The novel was about a love affair between a 17-year-old schoolgirl and a man old enough to be her father.

I was not surprised that Michael had a sister who was a successful author. Everyone in his circle seemed to be successful at something. I was surprised though that she wasn't more outgoing. When she gave me her hand she kept her eyes glued to the ground. During the meal she sat at another table with her back to me. A lot of beer and wine was drunk and most of us were drunk by the time we started dancing.

Towards morning a few of us were sitting around in Michael's room when one of the med students asked me about my acid trip. I was in a state of pleasant exhaustion, the result of several drunken highs. I had reached the mechanical doll stage. Whenever anyone asked me a question it wound me up and got me going.

It felt as though I talked about Amanda for hours. I told them everything I knew about her, how whenever there was something I didn't know, I'd ask Amanda and she would tell me. As usual I gave a precise and detailed account.

Then I buckled over onto the floor. Hands grabbed hold of me and carried me into my room down the hall.

When I woke I was nauseous and had a headache.

Unlike other people though, I like having a hangover. When you're feeling sick to your stomach and your head aches, depression seems to take a back seat.

The phone system at Nordisk Kollegium back in 1967 worked like this: First, the phone rang in the telephone booth downstairs in the student lounge. Then somebody went to your room and let you know there was a phone call for you. Then you went down to the phone booth from your own floor.

All this to explain that the trip to the telephone down the stairs from the third floor in the south wing to the phone was something I had done hundreds of times before. When I was told there was a call for me that afternoon in March 1967, I had no idea that it would change my life.

I picked up the receiver and heard a voice I hadn't heard before.

'Per Mortensen from Gyldendal Publishing Company.'

'Yes?'

'Am I speaking to Dan T. Moller? Dan T. Moller, studying dentistry?'

'Yes.'

'I'm calling to ask if you'd like to write a novel for us.'

'Excuse me, *what*?'

'A novel.'

'A *novel*?'

'You know what a novel is, don't you?'

'Yes, but I don't understand why we're talking about a novel. I'm studying to be a dentist.'

Someone laughed at the other end. 'Actually the novel is written already.'

'Is this some kind of sick joke? Who are you? Are the guys laughing their heads off someplace in the dorm?'

'Well, actually, there is someone in here listening.'

'Who?'

'Puk.'

'Who the hell is Puk?'

'Just a minute.'

I heard mumbling on the other end. Then a polished woman's voice came on the line.

'Dan?'

'Yes.'

'This is Puk Bonnesen.'

'Oh.'

'Don't you remember me?'

'Sure, Michael's little sister.'

'Dan, I'm not sure whether you'll be furious or grateful when you hear what I'm going to tell you.'

'Why should I be furious?'

'I'm really sorry if I've done anything wrong.'

'What have you done?'

'Ok, listen, promise you won't be terribly mad at me. Promise?'

'I'll be terribly mad at you if you don't tell me immediately what this is all about!'

'I recorded everything you said about Amanda on tape.'

'You did *what*? Are you out of your mind, you bitch?

What the hell were you thinking of? You recorded what I said about my depression when I was plastered?'

'That's exactly what I did. I've written it down and edited it. You've written a novel, Dan, whether you know it or not. My advice to you is to seriously calm down, read the novel and publish it. It will be quite a success.'

'Have you already written the *reviews* of a novel I didn't even know I wrote?'

'Yes, that's precisely what I'm trying to tell you, Dan.'

'What in the world made you do it?'

For the first time Puk fell silent for a few seconds on the other end. 'I'm sorry, I really don't know. Call it intuition, I think. Do you believe in intuition?'

'Intuition about what?'

'That you and I and two other people I know should consider a collaboration.'

'Are you planning my life now, Puk? Any more plans you'd like to pull out of the top hat?'

'Yes, actually there are. But you're upset so I suggest we terminate this fairly unpleasant conversation now in a civilised fashion.'

'Now what would a civilised fashion be?'

'It would involve your saying goodbye to me pleasantly whereupon you gently hang up.'

'Goodbye,' I snarled and hung up.

Puk Bonnesen had made plans. If I didn't realise it before, I did now. When Puk Bonnesen makes plans they're usually carried out, not because it would make her terribly unhappy if they weren't but because she had a knack for making plans people wanted to be part of. No one had ever called her a bitch before.

The Amanda book that they called a novel was published and well received. I took my final exams, graduated from dental school, and worked at a clinic on Odensegade in Osterbro for a year.

Before that I had met the two friends Puk had mentioned during our first telephone conversation. Nora From was 22 years old. Her first novel had been published the year before, launched as a satiric novel about love. The other was Boris Schauman, 23 years old. I knew him although he wasn't really part of the literary scene. He wrote poems, novels, short stories, and from the start his success had been phenomenal. He frequently appeared in newspapers and magazines and was a well known TV personality. He was called the mouthpiece of a generation, a divine talent. In addition he was very good-looking, with the brooding good looks of an old-fashioned romantic poet, which didn't make him any less charismatic.

The question I kept asking myself, but never said aloud, was: What on earth do they want from me?

I was sure two of the others, Nora From and Boris Schauman, were asking themselves the same question: What could we possibly want from a depressed dentist?

Puk Bonnesen knew exactly what she wanted from a depressed dentist although she'd never dream of saying so. As the polite, upper class girl she was, she would probably think it terribly impolite to explain it.

I didn't ask, afraid that the spell would be broken and I would be left alone in the woods.

I knew from the start that Puk and the two others had a powerful, anti-depressive effect on me. This wasn't because I felt especially comfortable in their company. For the most part I found them annoying, challenging, mocking, arrogant, downright hostile, in fact.

What did they want from me? I didn't know.

Our first project was a TV series for Danmarks Radio's youth division.

Puk had got the commission and brought in the three of us.

We rented an office on Rentemestervej in Norrebro. The furniture was ramshackle and the toilet didn't work most of the time. We used the toilet at the car repair workshop down the street.

From morning to night we were cooped up in a stuffy, little room sitting around a shaky round table, and together we wrote a TV series. I was still living at Nordisk Kollegium. I don't remember what my exact feelings for the others were. I do remember though that we were always bickering and belittling each other. What I remember most clearly is that from the moment we started work early in the morning I was almost depression-free. I found the three others arrogant, self-righteous, full of themselves, and not nearly as smart as they thought, but they kept depression at bay. That was what interested me. They were a powerful antidepressant.

FIVE

The Fiction Factory

I've known a number of depressed people. What they have in common is that it's hard for them to believe anyone could willingly hang out with them. How could anyone in his right mind be willing to spend time with somebody I can't stand myself?

Why Puk and her two friends would choose to sit with me in the same smoke-filled office day after day was something I only gradually came to understand over the years, but I had already glimpsed the answer the day we started work in the factory building on Rentemestervej in Norrebro.

In hindsight it should have been obvious from the start of our first collaboration, the children's television series in 12 episodes.

I knew nothing about TV, children didn't interest me, I had never written a word and especially not a drama.

The others had known for years that they were going to be writers. Puk was born into a family where writers were always coming and going. When she mentioned Knud, it was Knud Sonderby, Martin was Martin A. Hansen, Uncle Keld was Keld Abel.

Boris thought quite simply he was a born genius.

He thought God had reached down a hand into the two room apartment in Hvidovre where he lived with his parents who were post office employees. God had pointed his finger at Boris in his cradle and spoke. 'Unto this boy I bestow a special talent, a genius, to go forth and tell of his times and thereby go down in the history of Denmark.'

Nora didn't take things so seriously. She just wanted to have fun and have a good life. At school she was the gorgeous blonde that all the boys fell in love with. She had posters of Marilyn Monroe hanging on the walls of her room. She stood in front of the mirror for hours imitating Marilyn. 'Blondes just have more fun,' she would pout. But nobody ever took her for a dumb blonde. She had discovered she could make her classmates laugh while she was at Ingrid Jespersen School and was consequently assigned to writing the school play. If she could make other people laugh why not do it for a living? She had what the reviewers called a light touch and used it to amuse. She had no wish to change the world or analyse her own or anybody else's inner life very deeply. What she wanted was to entertain and that was the end of it.

As for me I wanted to be a dentist. The writers I had met during the course of my life had no appeal for me. They were insecure, self-promoting and, worst of all, poor. There wasn't an ounce of artistic ambition in me.

Yet here I was with three writers, with ambition coming out of their ears.

How could that be?

There was only one explanation. For unknown reasons this writing business had a tonic effect on me.

Puk was the one who had brought us together. Well mannered, upper class Puk was not in the least insecure, she was not self-promoting and she had absolutely no intention of being poor. Very early on she had made some decisions. She wanted to be a writer but she had no desire to scribble away alone in a garret. She needed a group, she was going to put together a team of colleagues. The group members would cover different areas but not be so different that they couldn't work together. She herself was an intellectual and politically engaged so she was looking for another woman who was just the opposite. She read one of Nora's satires in *Politiken* and saw one of her comedies performed at a small underground theatre and knew she was onto something. She biked out to where Nora lived with her parents on Peter Bangsvej and rang the bell.

'I'm Puk Bonnesen,' she said, when the door was opened. No one in the From family had ever heard of her.

Puk sat at the table where Mum and Dad and four children were having dinner. She sketched out her plan. Nora accepted immediately, particularly after Puk had said that the primary goal was to make money, lots of money.

Nora's father was a bank employee at Handelsbanken. He said later: 'Puk looked like a schoolgirl but she was so persuasive that I felt like quitting my job myself and going into partnership with her.'

It was Nora's idea that Boris Schauman should be the group's third man.

She had heard him read his poems aloud at the Students' Union. He was so absorbed in playing the divine poet with the tormented inner life that Nora was the only member of the audience that had found him pricelessly funny. 'Either that act is for real or it's the con of the century, in which case it's sublime.'

Boris was studying literary theory and lived at Regensen Hall of Residence. Puk and Nora headed for Rundetårn nearby and knocked on Boris' door. They were granted an audience. The great poet, wearing a striped bathrobe, looked thoughtfully out the window. He did his best to look world-weary although he was only twenty-one. He gave them to understand he had tried everything and was now weary of life.

He was willing to give them an autograph but then they would have to go. He was too busy to talk to all the female admirers beating down his door.

Puk and Nora looked at each other and had an idea. They quickly took off their clothes, stood in the middle of the room and told him he could do with them whatever he wanted. Their fondest wish was to bear his child, the child of a genius.

Boris gaped at them. His two admirers sat in his lap, one on each knee. Then they told him why they had come.

Boris accepted at once. 'But only if you swear you'll never pull a number like that on me again. Do you promise? Swear? Your breasts are the same size, did you know that? You really think we'll make money?'

It took them a long time to find the fourth member of the group. Nora said later: 'We agreed that the fourth member should be everything we weren't. He should be non-intellectual, without any particular talent, and utterly devoid of charm.'

I quickly grasped that it wasn't me they had chosen to be the fourth member of the group, it was Amanda. Amanda entered the picture the day we all met for the first time.

The meeting took place at the bus stop on Frederikssundsvej early one morning. The landlady of the office on Rentemestervej wanted to meet us there. She worked the night shift as a waitress. We could meet her at the bus stop when she came home from work at 5.30 am. The woman, whose name was Ruth Larsen, was late because she had just had a fight with her boyfriend. She had given him two black eyes and broken his nose. While this was going on we waited at the bus stop for an hour in the drizzling rain and had plenty of time to get to know each other.

'Did you bring Amanda?' was the first thing Boris said when we met.

'Of course I brought Amanda.'

'Is she wearing a raincoat?' Boris inquired.

'No, Amanda doesn't like raingear. She always carries an umbrella.'

'Has Amanda heard of me, Boris Schauman?'

'Of course Amanda has heard of you. Everybody in Denmark has heard of you, the brilliant young poet, the new Oehlenschläger, Drachmann, Frank Jæger, whoever.'

'Is Amanda as hostile as you are?'

'I'm not hostile. I'm just the messenger telling you what Amanda tells me.'

'Can I get to meet Amanda?' he asked.

'You're looking into her eyes as we speak.'

Boris stretched out a hand. 'Dan, the only thing I know about you is that you're a depressed dentist. Although being sentimental and banal isn't my style I'd like to take the opportunity to say straight out that I'm delighted to make your acquaintance.'

We shook hands.

Nora approached us. 'Oh, by the way my name is Nora From and I hate dentists. Therefore I hate you. Dentists are probably the most boring people I know, dentists talking about pension plans and retirement savings. You look so intense you really scare me. Can we be friends anyway?'

We shook hands.

Were the other three feeling what I was feeling? Were we all thinking the same thing as we stood there at the bus stop in the rain? That something unprecedented was happening in our lives. That from now on our lives would be divided into the time before the bus stop on Frederikssundsvej and the time after.

It was still unclear why they had chosen me but I was

vaguely aware of the stages leading up to the bus stop: Schroder himself; myself stretched out on the floor of the apartment on Strandboulevarden, tripping on acid; and especially Amanda, the woman who had emerged out of the acid shadows.

Amanda was the fifth member of the group. Nora and Boris wanted to know everything about her from the start. Without any doubt this was because Amanda could answer all their questions. No matter what they asked, the answer came promptly. Boris was sure I was having them on. Nora thought I must be seriously mentally ill if my depression was a woman who had an answer for everything. Puk said that for some strange reason my company and Amanda's gave her a sense of security.

'Secure?' snorted Boris. 'What's so secure about a depressed dentist and his sick imagination?'

'I can't imagine anything less threatening,' said Puk. 'That's why I suggested Dan as the fourth man. He suffers so much that the rest of us can breathe easy.'

We got to work at once on the TV series for Danmarks Radio Youth Entertainment Section. We hung a bulletin board on the wall on which we tacked our ideas for a scene.

The first time we got really stuck, our minds a blank and no ideas in sight, something occurred that would recur repeatedly in the future.

Nora suggested, 'Ask Amanda.'

Nora took out a sheet of paper on which she drew the outline of a woman's face. Within the outline she put a large question mark. She marched over to the bulletin board with the drawing and tacked it on.

We got up and took a break. We went outside. We walked around the neighborhood for an hour talking of other things. When we got back to the office Amanda had come up with three ideas. We couldn't use any of them but idea number three gave Nora another idea and the TV series took off from there.

Biking into town a few days later the three others started speculating about Amanda. Was Amanda an angel, a guardian angel, a secret friend or a worshipped idol? Boris claimed to be jealous of me because I had Amanda. Nora said she wanted a guardian angel, too. She knew who she would choose: Marilyn Monroe. Boris said that if he could have a guardian angel that was somebody dead he would choose someone who had died the same year as Marilyn Monroe, Ernest Hemingway. Puk opted for someone still alive and whom she had even met several times, Andy Warhol.

The next day they had all brought photos of their guardian angels. Next to Nora's drawing of Amanda hung photographs of Warhol, Monroe and Hemingway.

From that day on we were never at a loss. At the slightest hitch we would ask in unison, 'What does . . . say?' And then the name of one of the guardian angels would pop up.

Of course it didn't work every time, but it was fun. Or as Puk said, it gave us a sense of security.

We stayed together as a group after our time on

Rentemestervej. We rented rooms at different locations all over town, on Viborggade in Osterbro, on Gammel Koge Landevej, and in a disused bakery in Hvidovre.

Twice we rented a large open-plan office. Although our individual ways of writing were completely different the presence of the others posed no problem when we were working. Part of the time we worked as a group. We wrote films and TV series together, but mostly we worked alone on our own projects. After the Hvidovre bakery we bought an office condo on Gothersgade in central Copenhagen overlooking the Botanical Gardens.

For quite some time now we had been a company, a firm. The official name of the firm was The Factory of 21/9/1977, but we always referred to it as the Factory. The condo consisted of four offices, a kitchen and a communal room.

As usual Puk's vision formed the basis of the Factory's code of conduct.

The stated mission was to work hard, make money and especially to maintain a level of social intercourse that would keep us from getting on each other's nerves.

No guests were allowed at the Factory, especially no lovers or mistresses spending the night. No family, no husbands or wives, no kids. No dogs, no pets of any kind. No phones.

The general regulations and the rules governing the cleaning of the kitchen and bathroom including the sanctions imposed if the rules were broken were put in writing down to the last detail. The ultimate sanction consisted of having to invite the others to lunch at a venue in the immediate neighbourhood of Gothersgade.

Nora had formulated most of the rules that would keep us from getting on each other's nerves. She is almost obsessive when it comes to the rules of social intercourse and can discuss social codes for hours. In fact, this is the topic of all her plays, films, newspaper articles and books.

How to devise the rules and regulations that would regulate our interaction and keep us from getting fed up with each other or flying at each other's throats? That was the question. Some of us already knew writers. We had got to know others during the years we had been in business.

Nora drew up a long list of questions upon which her code of conduct would be based. Are writers more self-centred than other people? Yes, one would hope so. Vanity is the fuel that drives all writers. Are writers more combative than other people? Yes, one would hope so. Conflict lies at the core of all literature. Are writers more unlikable than other people? No, they don't have to be in order to survive. Are writers' egos bigger than other people's? One would hope so for their sake. Are writers better company than other people? No, they're just like anybody else. Some are fun, some are dull.

Nora answered all the questions herself and came up with the following rules:

We must not see each other socially.

We must not be friends with each other's families.

We must not under any circumstances have sex with each other.

We must never advise each other.

We must never divulge information about each other to anyone.

Of course we broke these rules frequently over the years but in principle we were in agreement.

Our collaboration at the Factory was going so well that all four of us were eager to safeguard it.

Of course we were friends with each other's families, but we rationed it. If one of us had a project that was going badly we would not normally ask each other for help, but there were exceptions just as there were when it came to personal problems. When a problem had reached the proportions of a stumbling block we could make an exception and turn to the others.

Nora called her rules Sympathy Management.

The Factory was to continue to be what it was, a factory, a factory for the production of letters, words, sentences, a fiction factory. Puk was the only one who primarily wrote non-fiction books, essays and journalism. The Factory's core product was fiction.

All the rules, regulations, precautionary measures and weekly meetings were originally devised to keep us from getting on each other's nerves. Then when the Factory had been in existence for a number of years we expanded into an area none of us had imagined at the start. The rule not to divulge information about each other to third parties became a legally binding confidentiality agreement. Puk was the best known of us and the one who knew everyone who was anyone in intellectual and artistic circles. She began to receive feelers from publishers and writers. Could she read a manuscript completely anonymously and give an opinion as to what could be done to save it? A businessman wanted to write his autobiography and was willing to pay Puk to help him in secret. A best-selling author had had a breakdown. Could Puk confidentially help the publisher finish her last novel? Puk was offered so much work of that kind that she started dividing it up between the three of us without telling anyone.

We got the system up and running risk-free and the offers for covert work kept pouring in. So did the payments.

All four of us worked hard. We liked working. We liked making money. The confidential work was often fun because the secrecy involved imparted a certain sense of freedom. The fact that it was so well paid made it even more fun of course. Anonymity can be a great spur to creativity.

Everything went through Puk. She divided the jobs among us. The first speeches she was commissioned to write she wrote herself: after dinner speeches, birthday speeches, funeral elegies. The demand for speeches she had written was so great that she started passing commissions to the rest of us. If the speech was supposed to be funny, Nora got it. If it was supposed to be emotional, Boris got it. If it was going to be given by someone with a mental disorder I got it.

This kind of work sometimes involved a personal meeting, which always took place in the Botanical Gardens, the park on the other side of the street. The Gardens were originally Boris' idea. Anything that could get his creative spark fired up appealed to him. Basically all four of us were producers of fiction.

The Botanical Gardens was the obvious setting for all kinds of fiction, fantasies, dreams, play. We became ardent supporters of the Botanical Gardens. Boris was the first and wrote a collection of poems about them. Nora wrote a romantic novel in which all the illicit encounters took place there. Puk discussed the garden as an image of order and harmony. I restricted myself to making a depression study of the garden.

A Botanical Garden with all its plants has an effect on a certain kind of depression. When I wander through the garden my depression barometer clearly registers fluctuations. My story was called 'The Botanic Gardens Seen through the Eyes of a Depressed Person'. As soon as it was finished I stuffed it into my desk drawer; I write about depression as little as possible.

On the rare occasions when we wrote messages or letters to each other over the years our favorite topics were 1) the Botanical Gardens and 2) our guardian angels. It started out as a game and later we toyed with the idea of collaborating on a book, 'Tales of the Botanical Gardens'.

On the bulletin board in the kitchen were pictures of our four guardian angels, Warhol, Monroe, Hemingway, and Amanda. Next to them photos of the Botanical Gardens began to appear regularly. We vied with each other to know the most about the garden and its plants.

We didn't spend much time together except when we were collaborating on a project, either a TV series or a film. This was something we looked forward to although we were all in agreement that our being together needed to be rationed.

Boris somewhat grandly called it the 'love diet'.

Nora said, 'If I spend too much time with you guys I get talent constipation.'

Puk said, 'We have to be able to stand each other all our lives.'

I said nothing. Mostly because I hadn't thought of anything worth saying.

When we weren't on the diet we got to work at 8 a.m. and left at 5 p.m. We sat in the kitchen or, in Boris' case, stretched out on the floor. In the middle of the day we took a stroll in the Botanical Gardens.

Boris was Ernest Hemingway, the macho writer with the built-in bullshit detector. Puk was Andy Warhol, a machine pumping out literary products on the assembly line. Nora was Marilyn Monroe, soft and beautiful whose only aim was to please. I was Amanda, my depression.

Amanda had long since become an intimate acquaintance of the other three. Not only did they know a great deal about her, they also held her in high esteem.

There was a very simple reason. Every time we ran out of gas and the way ahead looked blocked, one of them would always say, 'What does Amanda say?' When Amanda couldn't provide an immediate answer she and I crossed the street to the Botanical Gardens and wandered around for as long as it took.

For reasons that seemed mysterious to me at the time, and still seem mysterious, Amanda always came up with an answer. The answer was not always the solution to our problems but it invariably set a reaction off in one of us that led to the right solution.

Monroe, Warhol and Hemingway were always willing to contribute but they couldn't touch Amanda.

Puk had an explanation. The three guardian angels all had depression; Amanda *was* depression itself.

SIX

The Telephone Rings on Strandboulevarden

At Nordisk Kollegium there were student societies you could join. Two law students I played soccer with put me up for membership of the society called The Cup.

The associations occasionally held soccer tournaments against each other. One evening during one such tournament I was called to the phone during the break. 'Dan Moller! Dan Moller to the phone!'

'Dan Moller? I'd like to speak to Dan Moller.'

'Speaking.'

A voice I didn't know was on the other end.

'Are you Dan Thorvald Moller?'

'I am.'

'My name is Beate.'

'And?'

'Do you remember me?'

'Do we know each other?'

'We met last time at the funeral.'

'Whose funeral?'

'I'm Ib Schroder's daughter.'

'Doesn't he have five daughters?'

'Four.'

'Four daughters, three sons and how many wives?'

'Is that supposed to be funny?'

'Not at all.'

'You sound just as annoying as you look.'

'Now I know who you are. You're the youngest daughter, the one that lived with Schroder in the apartment on Vester Voldgade.'

'Have you ever been here?'

'No.'

'My father said you were depressed like him.'

'Not *wasn't* depressed. I *am* depressed.'

'God, you're annoying. Are you always wagging your finger at somebody?'

'Yes, actually. How did you guess?'

'I know your type. A couple of them are my teachers at High School.'

'I remember you. You're the one that looks like a boy.'

'No, that's my sister. I'm the one that looks like a dog.'

'I think that was a supposed to be a joke, right?'

'My father said you're totally devoid of a sense of humor. Is that correct?'

'Yes, but I try to laugh in the right places.'

'My brothers and sisters and their wives and husbands and mothers are ransacking the apartment. If you want to see the papers my father told you about, you better get over here soon.'

'When can I come?'

'Come tonight if you can. It's ok if it's late. I can't sleep anyway, I'm so furious at my sisters and brothers.

They're hauling away all the furniture and paintings. You don't have a shotgun, do you?'

'Sure I've got a shotgun, right here in the dorm. I'll take it with me and mow down your sisters and brothers with pellets.'

'That was almost funny, Dan.'

'Unintentionally.'

Just before midnight I leaned my bike against the wall of the apartment building on Vester Voldgade where Schroder used to live.

When I reached the fifth floor the door was open. I went in. A girl who did in fact look like a boy came out into the hall. She stretched out her hand and I shook it.

'Beate Schroder,' she said.

'Dan Moller.'

'So that's what you look like.'

'Didn't you say you'd seen me before?'

'No, I never said that.'

'I've never seen you before either.'

'How can I be sure you're Dan Moller?'

'I took my passport with me as well as the shotgun, of course.'

'How old are you?'

'22. How old are you?'

'I'll be 18 soon.'

'In other words you're 17.'

'Are you always so annoying in that particularly infuriating way?'

'No, I've got a lot of different ways of being annoying.'

'When will you graduate from dental school?'

'In two years.'

'I'll be starting there in the fall.'

'Isn't your mother a dentist too? A professor in Stockholm, right?'

'So you do know who I am.'

'Your father said you're the child that resembles him most.'

'Apart from the fact that I'm the opposite of depressed.'

'What's the opposite of depressed?'

'You should be the first to know.'

'I do know. I'd just like to hear the words you use.'

'I'm happy. I've decided to be happy all my life.'

'I think that's an extremely sensible decision.'

'Come into the dining room. I've got all my father's papers together for you.'

The light was on in all the rooms. The apartment was almost empty.

The dining room was piled with papers and letters, all written by hand with a fountain pen.

Schroder's daughter explained: 'All of it's about depression. I tried reading some of it, but I didn't understand a word. The letters are part of his correspondence with someone abroad, they're almost all about depression.'

'What do you want me to do?' I asked.

'I don't want you to do anything. My father decided you should be allowed to look through it.'

'Did you speak to him about it?'

'He didn't tell me he was going to kill himself.'

She turned on her heel and left the room.

I took off my jacket, hung it on the back of a chair and went to work.

Schroder had written about depression on all different kinds of paper. A lot if it was jotted down on small scraps, often on the back of bills from the grocer, the butcher or the fish store. In addition there were small notebooks he had filled with his thoughts on the subject. He had sorted the letters by sender, and bundled and bound them together with a rubber band.

In the light of the large chandelier I set out to see if I could find some kind of system. I couldn't. All I could do was plunge in at some arbitrary point. It was obvious how these scraps had come into existence: Schroder had an idea while he was in a shop. To make sure he didn't forget he had jotted it down. The handwriting was often illegible but gradually I got to know it so well I could read it.

Shortly after 4 a.m. I left the apartment. I didn't know where his daughter was.

The next night I came back, shortly before midnight again. Beate was packing. We only exchanged a few words.

I kept this up for a week until I had a good, general idea of what was in the papers.

Every word was about something that had occupied me 24 hours a day for my entire life. I was in familiar territory, but I still had to reread much of it a number of times before I could begin to make out even the barest outline.

63

I needed to mobilise everything I had discussed with Schroder in order to understand his terminology. We had talked about pharmacology and corrective jaw surgery, but mostly we had discussed depression for hours on end.

He was a generation older than I, and had given the subject much more thought than I had, but I had come up with some ideas that interested him. My description of the kind of depression I suffered from didn't correspond to his own, but there were elements that overlapped and the terminology I used to describe it intrigued him.

One day, walking down Norrebrogade, we had tossed around the idea of collaborating on a study of the kind of depression he called signal depression. He believed it was what we both suffered from.

Now that he was dead and I sat there reading the papers he had left behind it was as if I could hear him saying, 'It's up to you now to carry out our plans, Dan. I'm sorry I couldn't go the distance. Use whatever you can here, my papers, my thoughts, my life.'

During the weekends when I didn't have any classes to go to, I spent all of Saturday and Sunday in the apartment on Vester Voldgade.

Schroder's other children took turns dropping in with their spouses and fighting with Beate. They yelled and screamed and accused each other of the most heinous things. Cups and plates flew through the air in the kitchen. Now and then someone came running through the dining room where I was sitting.

At first they would comment on me. 'Who the hell is that guy over there?'

They didn't wait for an answer but continued to ransack and raid.

A woman who introduced herself as Ib Schroder's Wife Number Three waved to me and called, 'If you find any letters from me, then for God's sake hurry up and destroy them.'

'Why?'

'I used to write him pornographic letters he could masturbate to when I was on a business trip. So he wouldn't be unfaithful.'

An older brother dashed through the dining room saying, 'I'm David, I couldn't get you to kill Beate, could I?'

'Why?'

'She thinks she's an only child and the old man's sole heir.'

'The old man being Ib Schroder?'

'I am *so* furious at him for committing suicide.'

Late Sunday night I was alone in the apartment. Beate had gone to the movies with her boyfriend.

All the papers pertaining to what Schroder had called signal depression lay in a pile in front of me.

Most of it had been written long before we met. Nevertheless it was as though a lot of it had been written directly to me. The 'you' he was writing to could easily have been myself. He was striving hard to understand it. He simplified. He made diagrams, explaining it as if to a child. As he said.

It was not a full-fledged theory of depression. It was an attempt to establish a foundation for a theory.

I had been so deeply engrossed by his papers for such a long time that I seemed to hear him talking to me directly. He was confident I understood every word he said.

I quickly wrote down my own comments on the theories he had come up with. I was so absorbed that I didn't notice Beate had come home. When she put her hand on my shoulder I was so startled I dropped my pen.

'Sorry,' she said.

That's ok. How was the movie?'

'I didn't see much of it because my boyfriend and I were making out most of the time.'

'You have the whole apartment to make out in. Why do it at the movies?'

'There! That's *exactly* what my father would have said! And you said it *exactly* the same way!'

'Is that good or bad?'

'It's just an observation.'

'Were you fond of your father?'

'I loved my father. I still love him.'

'That's terrible.'

'Why is it terrible?'

'You love your father and now he's dead.'

'It's not *you* it's terrible for, it's me,' she pointed out.

'Maybe that was what I was trying to say.'

'Why didn't you then?'

'All sweetness and light tonight, aren't we, little Beate?

You've been making out in the movies and you look like you're ready to kill someone.'

'Don't you know why?'

'No.'

'Have you read the letters too? Especially from that American my father corresponded with?'

'No I haven't gotten to them yet.'

'He's a writer. His name is Salinger. I read that book of his, *The Catcher in the Rye*.'

'What made you say that, that I should know why?'

'Why what?'

'Why you feel like killing me.'

'My father met Salinger during the war.'

'Why don't you answer?'

'They were in the hospital together and met a girl called Esmé.'

'You know what, Beate, this conversation is confusing me.'

'It's not a conversation.'

'What is it then?'

'Don't you even know that?'

'Know what?'

'Why don't you kiss me?'

'Why should I kiss you?'

'That's what I asked you, you jerk.'

'Weren't you at the movies all night making out with your boyfriend?'

'He's not my boyfriend anymore.'

'Can I kiss you?'

'Yes.'

'Well I'll be damned.'

'Have you given any thought as to whether you *feel* like kissing me?'

'No.'

'Well, do.'

'I have.'

'Do you?'

'Yes, I think it's a great idea.'

'We'll kiss here first, then we'll go lie on my bed and kiss some more.'

'I think that's a great idea too.'

She sat on my lap and we kissed for a long time. Then we did what Beate said. We lay on her bed, took off our clothes and kissed some more.

SEVEN

Sex and Depression

Sex has always been one of my main interests. I'm no different from anyone else that way. But if you're depressed, your sex life is depressed too, and that's a subject only a person with depression could find interesting.

Depressive sex usually involves masturbation and bad sex, neither of which anyone with depression would ever dream of knocking.

As a masturbator I've always been a large scale consumer of pornography. As a depressed masturbator I've always been on the lookout for antidepressant porn.

Until I was 22 my sex life consisted of masturbation and bad sex. People with depression are experts at bad sex. Sadly, most depressed people are usually nowhere near getting even bad sex. If they do, they think: Better bad sex than no sex.

Fortunately the depressed and the non-depressed have equal access to the pornography needed for masturbation.

The sex shops divide their wares by category. There's ordinary sex, and there are all kinds of sub- categories: sex with leather and whips, SM, sex with blacks, sex with Asians, and so on. There are no shelves for sex for the depressed. We have to put together our own category. This tallies well with the fact that no two types of depression are alike. That's why certain kinds of sex have an antidepressant effect on one kind of depression but can aggravate others.

Most people with depression feel tense about life and almost always have a complicated sex life. Their attitude towards sex is non-spontaneous. They envy anyone who can have sex spontaneously; sex is something other people want and do without thinking about it much. People with depression brood and speculate over their sex lives before they even get *near* sex.

I was convinced I would never have anything that even slightly resembled a normal sex life. I would end my days as a depressed masturbator. I was pretty sure I knew why too: my eyes. You want to look at the person you're having sex with. If you don't look at that person then it's not sex, it is masturbation. But when your eyes are open you allow the other person to look inside you. Inside me was something neither girls nor women wanted to see, depression. It scared them. Nothing is so unsexy.

The first time I let a woman look inside me was when I spent the night with Beate Schroder in the apartment on Vester Voldgade. The first time I had non-disastrous sex with a woman was that same night with Beate Schroder on Vester Voldgade. I kept my eyes open. This had never happened before. I let her look inside me. She saw nothing frightening. Her reaction was, 'That's what people with depression look like inside. No big deal.'

Depressed people spend a lot of time brooding and

turning things over in their minds. They have daydreams, they have wishes for the future. What they long for most of all is for the depression to go away. They want what everyone wants: love.

I dreamt of finding love too, but I had given up hope long ago. Whenever I fell in love it always ended badly. Girls and women liked me until they found out how knotted up and tense I was inside.

I had finally met someone who thought I was perfectly normal. What went on inside me was perfectly recognisable so there was no reason to get upset about it. It was normal, everyday behavior to her; she had lived with her father her whole life.

I wasn't cured, I was still depressed; I agonised over every tiny detail in my life. But whenever Beate Schroder and I lay there in her bed on Vester Voldgade kissing each other I knew that I had taken a giant step towards finding what I always called the *enzyme*.

The enzyme is what I call the small mechanism in my brain that's out of balance and causes my depression.

The scientific breakthrough was not the fact that for the first time in my life I was engaging in something that resembled ordinary sex. It was not the fact that it had been arousing to watch Beate undress in the light of the street lamp. It was not the fact that our nipples touched. It was not the intense pleasure I experienced placing my hands on top of her buttocks.

No, the real step forward on the road to the enzyme lay spread out on the table in the dining room, in the

71

piles of handwritten papers Schroder had left behind. I had finally read the letters Salinger had written Schroder, and there discovered the germ of what I had spent my entire life trying to find out.

When I met Schroder we quickly discovered that we suffered from similar types of depression. He had spent the major part of his life mapping out the form he suffered from. He applied the same scientific approach as when he was working with corrective jaw surgery and pharmacology. Now he had left his notes to me. He had met Salinger in Germany during the war at a hospital where they had both been admitted for nervous break-downs; Salinger suffered from depression, too. They had discovered they suffered from similar types of depression and remained in contact after the war. Now Salinger's letters were on the desk and Beate and I were on her bed.

I had gone through the letters and Schroder's notes several times in the course of the many hours I spent in the apartment on Vester Voldgade. The picture of a certain type of depression was beginning to take shape. Schroder and Salinger had tried together to define the type of depression they both suffered from. They wrote about other things too. They told each other what was going on in their lives, but depression was the leitmotif of their correspondence. In one of his earliest letters to Salinger, Schroder suggested half in jest that they call their type of depression the Salinger Syndrome. Salinger responded by proposing they call the treatment they were seeking together the Kierkegaard Cure.

Kierkegaard was depressed. He called it melancholy. Depression is a leitmotif in all his writing. Schroder and Salinger agreed that the best description of their depression could be found in Kierkegaard's sentence: 'Anxiety is a sympathetic antipathy and an antipathetic sympathy.'

The sentence described a certain type of depression and the rudiments of a treatment, they felt.

Salinger had a special relationship to Denmark because he had read Kierkegaard as a young man. During a certain period of his life he had planned to read Kierkegaard in the original. He had started studying Danish but had given it up. In one of his early letters to Schroder he wrote that Kierkegaard was the person that had most accurately described his own state of mind. Schroder had an older brother who was a clergyman and a Kierkegaard expert, and Kierkegaard became a recurring element in the correspondence between Salinger and Schroder. The two men set out to identify the components that constitute the Salinger Syndrome and the Kierkegaard Cure based on what Kierkegaard said about sympathetic antipathy and antipathetic sympathy.

I had read Salinger but now I reread him with fresh eyes. This time I could hear a voice, a narrative voice, addressing me directly. He was writing about something I knew all too well, a certain form of hidden depression.

For me all his books were written by a person with depression; I knew that kind of depression. At one point in *The Catcher in the Rye* the main character says that a writer should be someone you feel like knocking on his door and talking to. Salinger lived in the States so he was in no danger of that from me. I knew from the newspapers that he had shut himself off from the rest of the world. He gave no interviews, lived far away from New York, surrounded by secrecy, and no reader ever knocked on his door.

I didn't knock on his door; I wrote him a letter. I related the facts surrounding Ib Schroder's death, and spoke of Kierkegaard.

Kierkegaard appears in Salinger's work in various contexts, and not without reason. Kierkegaard's melancholy is closely related to Salinger's.

My kind of depression was closely related to Salinger's and Kierkegaard's.

In my second letter I was guilty of a lie, a white lie. My excuse was that Salinger's letters had had an antidepressant effect on me and I wanted to make sure the medicine kept coming. So I waved a carrot in front of him, the carrot being Kierkegaard. I wrote that I had been weaned on Kierkegaard since my uncle was one of the greatest Kierkegaard experts in Denmark.

Salinger reported on his own melancholy temperament. He never mentioned the word depression. I saw a connection between what he said about himself and Kierkegaard's melancholy, and my own.

I always looked forward to Salinger's antidepressant letters and did my best to keep the correspondence headed in the right direction. I included tidbits of Kierkegaard lore in every letter. Salinger was interested in Kierkegaard and I was interested in Salinger.

I had another reason for being interested in him apart from the antidepressant effect of his letters: We exchanged ideas for keeping depression at bay. In addition to the remedies we devised together, my letters contained my own personal contributions towards what we called the Kierkegaard Cure. This was practical advice on treating a certain form of depression, all of which I maintained was to be found in Kierkegaard's writings.

The Kierkegaard Cure consisted partly of material for which there actually was supporting evidence in Kierkegaard's works and partly of material I had thought up myself. You could call it fraud, pure fantasy or an attempt at Kierkegaard exegesis. At any rate one thing was certain: Salinger kept up the correspondence because of the Kierkegaard Cure.

In order to make sure I was on solid ground I started studying Kierkegaard, particularly the passages that deal with anxiety, or angst. I soon came to believe that this applied to most of his work. I contacted Kierkegaard scholars who were experts on Kierkegaard and anxiety. They received me warmly. A few of them suffered from depression themselves. I never tried to conceal the fact that I was depressed, too. I never mentioned Salinger's name. I told them I was looking to Kierkegaard for help in trying to understand the philosophical aspects of depression.

The more depressed the Kierkegaard scholars were, the more powerful was their antidepressant effect on me. Putting into words what I had discovered and sending it to Salinger in the States had the same effect.

75

My correspondence with Salinger filled a large part of my life. First, there was the physical pleasure of writing the letters. Then there was the joy of imagining him walking down to his mailbox at the side of the road in Cornish, New Hampshire. I had seen photos of that mailbox in Time Magazine. It was an iconic mailbox. No photographer had ever succeeded in catching Salinger picking up his mail. How and when he did it remained a mystery.

When I got a letter from Salinger I left it on my desk unopened for at least 24 hours. It was a pleasure I wished to savour to the full.

I tried to imagine what Salinger would do when he got my letters. Did he open them immediately? Did he open them with his finger or a letter opener? Did he read them standing up or sitting down? Did he tell anyone about them? Did he tell his wife or kids, 'I've got a letter from that dentist in Copenhagen I told you about, that Kierkegaard expert. He sends me all kind of information, research, gossip, about my absolutely favorite philosopher. Remember that guy from Denmark I was in the hospital with in Germany during the war? He's the boyfriend of his daughter now.'

I never mentioned the letters to anyone myself.

He wrote very little about his private life. He said he worked every day but strongly doubted he would ever publish any of it. Publishing a book was too great a violation of his privacy, he said.

I described to him the anatomy of my depression.

What I was suffering from was an imbalance of the

sensory processing system. All impressions hit me directly with an immediate, devastating effect. Nothing was filtered off. I was bombarded with impressions just like everybody else, but in my case the external pressure was too high, it blasted me. To protect myself from the shock wave I created a negative pressure inside, a depression.

Depression is a defence. You have to protect yourself from the mass of impressions weighing you down, otherwise you'll be crushed.

Most people whose filter is out of balance protect themselves by erecting an internal wall. They shield themselves from an overload of impressions, but behind the wall they're in pain, they're lonely. Cowering behind the wall, they cut themselves off from what they need most: friendship, attention, love.

If you don't learn how to get out from behind the wall once in a while you're in danger of dying of malnutrition.

Salinger wrote back that there were parts of what I said that he recognised.

I've spent my whole life studying the form of depression that Schroder and Salinger called the Salinger Syndrome, trying to find a remedy. Salinger gives the best description of depression in his stories. Kierkegaard gives the best philosophical interpretation. My job was to figure out a practical treatment, and I needed Salinger's help.

The various types of depression fascinate me, first of all my own, of course; I want to understand it and fight it. But other people's depression interests me too, particularly the hidden kind, the undetected kind. Depression comes in many varieties. My own form is so obvious that I've always known it was there. There are other types that are either disguised or invisible or transparent.

I've met many people with depression and I've compared many different types of depression. No two depressions are alike for the very simple reason that depression strikes an individual and no two individuals are alike.

Curing your own depression is a virtually impossible task. It takes time and energy. You enter a boundless universe and most of the time you're working in the dark. Doubt is your constant companion. You have to figure everything out for yourself.

When I look at myself – and I look at myself constantly 24 hours a day – I see myself as a research scientist who has spent his entire life studying one little enzyme. In my case I've spent my whole life studying one little mechanism. My life consists of a multitude of unconnected details, fragments. What connects them is Amanda, Depression.

Many years before, Schroder had tried to explain to his daughter what being depressed felt like. To make it easier to understand he illustrated it by making drawings. The drawings were among the papers he left behind. One of the drawings was of a post office. Underneath the post office he had written: 'Let's say you receive lots and lots of mail all the time and you don't know what to do with it. Some of it might be important and should be read immediately, some of it can wait, some of it's just spam and you can throw it away. But the mail keeps piling up and you don't know what to do.

'At the post office they have a mail processing system, a mail sorter. Well, I don't have that kind of filter. I'm in danger of drowning in mail, suffocating in mail. When I feel I'm drowning in mail I'm unhappy. That's what depression is: When you feel you're being swamped with mail.'

The post office was in bed with me when I slept with Beate. Beate had understood about the post office since she was a child and Schroder had explained it to her. I recognized Schroder's description at once; it corresponded perfectly with my own type of depression. My own post office simply didn't work.

I wanted to study the Salinger Syndrome more closely. I knew nothing of the Kierkegaard Cure as yet. Schroder had just made me a gift of it. He had also given me his daughter. Beate was the first woman I slept with who could understand what I meant if I said my post office was out of order.

But now, lying in bed with Beate in the apartment on Vester Voldgade, my post office was open for business. All mail relating to Beate's face, her voice, her body was received and opened immediately. My post office was up and running for the first time.

It had taken me 22 years to discover ordinary sex. I was aware that I had been luckier than I had ever dreamed and I knew it was a stroke of luck that comes once in a lifetime.

Beate was dangerous for me, I knew that from the start. From now on there would be a life with Beate and a life without Beate. That's what I call dangerous.

EIGHT

Broome Street, New York, April 1987

On the stroke of 9 a.m. a light brown Chrysler drew up in front of the Pioneer Hotel on Broome Street where we were waiting. Rose Goldman was behind the wheel. Art jumped out and opened the door for us.

The trip to New Hampshire through upper New York State and New England took place in a cheerful, chatty atmosphere for all the world as though Art and Rose were our American hosts who wanted to show us the beauties of New England's gentle spring landscape.

Not a single mention was made of Salinger, an appointment, an interview, a letter transfer.

They had brought homemade sandwiches and a thermos of tea and coffee. They spoke of their lives, their families and friends, and we spoke of ours. Rose had once sung in a trio when she was at college. She knew all the songs of the 60s and her Diana Ross impersonation singing 'You can't hurry love' with Beate was a huge success.

Was Salinger waiting for us at his home in Cornish? Or would he meet us at a drugstore or a restaurant in town? Art and Rose apparently didn't know either because as we approached our destination they engaged in lengthy phone conversations with people whose names we didn't catch. It sounded as if they were receiving instructions; their contribution to the conversation consisted almost solely of 'Yes' and 'I understand' and 'Sure'.

When we reached Cornish, Art turned into the parking lot behind a supermarket. He found a parking space between two trucks and turned off the ignition. In silence we began to wait. Suddenly a woman knocked on the car door. She had strawberry blonde hair and was in her late 30s. She and Art had a brief exchange which we couldn't hear after which the woman disappeared among the parked cars. Art switched on the ignition and drove out of the parking lot. A small blue Japanese car passed us when we were out on the main road. The strawberry blonde was at the wheel. Art followed her as she drove out of town. She drove very fast for a while and then after about 10 minutes made a sharp left. We entered a wooded area. At the end of a long forest road, in a clearing, an old black Land Rover was parked. The woman drew up alongside. A man got out of the Land Rover. He was tall, his thick hair dark and greying. He wore glasses.

It was him. I recognized him at once. He was wearing a pair of blue canvas trousers and a blue sweater. A light coloured silk kerchief was tied loosely around his neck. He was elegantly and neatly dressed. It was him, the man I had dreamed of meeting, J.D. Salinger himself.

The woman indicated I should get out of the car. I went over to Salinger who greeted me pleasantly. His handshake was firm. He had an old man's hands.

He was 67 years old but well preserved. He looked at me kindly and searchingly. His eyes were jet black and his eyelashes, which so many women had fallen for I had read somewhere, were still thick and attractive.

The woman got into the driver's seat of the black Land Rover. Salinger invited me to get into the back seat with him. As he was getting in I heard his voice for the first time. Mellow and pleasant, the way he must have sounded ever since he was a young man, I thought.

The first thing he said was that he was hard of hearing, but he had recently acquired a hearing aid made in Denmark, that he was very satisfied with. He asked the woman, whom he called Colleen, to start driving. Out of the rear window I could see my wife standing in the clearing, growing smaller and smaller. I felt like a schoolboy leaving his parents for the first time, watching them disappear from the back seat of the bus.

For as long as the interview lasted we drove around the country roads near Cornish. All I was aware of was the old man sitting next to me. In his own way he was just as handsome as the only existing official pictures. I gaped, hypnotised.

There was something attractive and frightening about him at the same time. He had a way of pushing his jaw out and staring fixedly at me that made him look like Marlon Brando playing Don Vito Corleone, the Godfather himself. Mafia associations, literary mafia, were not unwarranted; Salinger was the boss of his own universe. He demanded obedience and omertà, total silence. He had made me an offer through a strawman. Now I had broken mafia rules by outbidding him with an offer he could have refused, but which he had chosen to accept.

'Let's get started,' said Salinger.

'Are you the one that wants to buy the letters?'

'Does that surprise you?'

'Why didn't you just write me in Denmark and ask for them back?'

'Would you have given them to me?'

'Of course'

'Even when you know how much money is involved.'

'Hmm. I hope so.'

'Collectors would give their eye teeth to get a hold of those letters. Everything I think about Kierkegaard is in there.'

'How do you feel about my blackmailing you into giving me your first real interview?'

'I have mixed feelings about it, very mixed, but I've made a promise. A deal is a deal. I'm doing it because of Kierkegaard. I've been obsessed with Kierkegaard ever since I read him for the first time at military school. Everything I've ever written was inspired by Kierkegaard.'

'Was that why you answered my first letter, back then?'

'Yes. And also because you knew things about Kierkegaard only a Dane could tell me. Holden Caulfield is partly based on Kierkegaard, partly on my own life.

The way Holden divides other people into categories, those he doesn't like, the phonies, and those he likes, is straight out of Kierkegaard when he speaks of the single individual and the ethical and aesthetic idiosyncracy which so painfully cuts him off from the world and from living a normal life. That's Holden's dilemma, it was Kierkegaard's, and it's mine.'

'Why do you care where your letters end up? What's so terrible about a collector or a university?'

'Are you naive or do you just pretend to be?'

'I just pretend.'

'When I was young I dated Oona O'Neill. I was crazy about her and her best friend, Carol, who later married the writer, William Saroyan, and after that the actor, Walther Matthau. When Oona started going with Charlie Chaplin I wrote her a bunch of letters. I was devastated and I ridiculed Charlie Chaplin. Those letters are now in the possession of a university library. Anyone can just go in and read them! Somebody even tried to publish them as a book, but my lawyers managed to put a stop to that.'

'Do you think I should feel like a traitor, a whore or just a common blackmailer for taking advantage of the situation to get an interview with you?'

'You'll get no absolution from me! But I know what I'm expected to deliver. I've been a devoted fan of lots of people myself.'

'You? The guy that's famous for refusing to let his fans anywhere near him?'

'There are people I would have travelled halfway around the world just to see walk down the street.'

'Who?'

'The person I'm the biggest fan of is Kierkegaard but he died in 1855 so that pretty much leaves him out, I guess. The other person I worshipped just as much as groupies dote on film stars and rock singers was Freud. I besieged him with letters and I met him once too.'

'How did that come about?'

'I wrote to Freud in Vienna when I was young. He always answered me, kindly and impersonally. He got lots of fan mail. I thought he was a brilliant novelist, in Kierkegaard's class. His works on the mysteries of the soul were pure poetry to me. I dreamed of meeting him. Just before the war broke out I went to London to meet him. I was relentless. I *had* to meet him. I went to where he was living in exile and knocked on the door. And there he was, the old man, almost a dotard, his mouth in excruciating pain because of the cancer. He listened patiently to what I said, how much I admired him, how much it meant to me to meet him. My secret wish was to get to touch him, physically touch him. I was sure some kind of spiritual energy would be transferred from him to me by the least physical contact. Freud invited me to walk with him in the garden. We strolled there together, arm and arm, for 10 minutes at most without saying a word, Freud leaning on me for support. I was ecstatic. When his daughter Anna called Freud into the house again I did something perhaps I should be ashamed of.

I stole a small plant shoot and put it into a little plastic bag I had brought. I took such good care of that shoot that its descendants now live in my garden. The day that plant dies I'll die too, I'm sure of it.'

'So you understand us, all us fans.'

'Otherwise I wouldn't know what I was turning down, would I? And who was a greater fan than Kierkegaard? He wallowed in names, he hid behind any number of pseudonyms the way only people do who long to be famous. He sat at Hegel's feet in Berlin, he dreamt of knowing everyone who was anyone in Copenhagen and was beside himself with rage when he wasn't invited to the right parties. Kierkegaard was the ultimate fan long before the word was invented. A fan wants names, a steady flow of names to root around in so as to fill up the emptiness inside. I'm offering you a trade in names to get my letters back. You want names, facts. Don't get me wrong though. I don't mean to imply you're a pig!'

'I'm surprised you don't sound angry.'

'Listen, you Kierkegaard landsman. I've been friends with some of the most notorious gossips in the world. Take Truman Capote and Andy Warhol for example.'

'You were friends with Warhol? And he never said anything about it in his diaries?'

'Andy virtually besieged me. He told me he looked up people who knew me, he came up here and knocked on the door. Andy taught me something. Unfortunately it was much too late at that point; I was already famous as the freak who never gave interviews. Andy taught me how to be open and reserved at the same time. There was Andy the exhibitionist, wide open, the persona he had created as a shelter from the outside world. And there was the shy, withdrawn Andy. He kept that side of himself to himself. That way he didn't have to live the hermit's life I had created for myself. I'm just as sociable as Andy was, or at least almost. It's just that Andy managed his inner split better than me. We were good friends. He used to come up here and visit, especially after he had been shot in the stomach by that crazy woman who wanted some of his fame to wear off on her and could only get it by shooting him. When Andy was here he took off his wig so nobody recognized him. We'd go fishing together. Andy was extremely intelligent and enjoyed hiding behind the façade of the red-neck village idiot. On the personal level the person he reminded me of most was Elvis Presley.'

'Did you know Elvis too? I thought you despised popular culture?'

'Does that surprise you? We often spoke on the phone. He was very gentle, very well mannered.'

Salinger fell silent for a moment. Then he turned to me and indicated I could continue the interview.

'Do you still write?'

'Every day.'

'What do you do with your manuscripts? Is it true what the rumours say that you have a safe full of manuscripts that won't be published until you die?'

'I've published lots of books since 1965.'

'You what?'

'Under other names.'

'How many?'

'Seven. Or is it eight?'

'Can you give me the books' titles?'

'I can. But I won't.'

'Why don't you publish them under your own name?'

'It turned out that publishing under a pen name has a marvelous effect on me. The vanity, the ego I've been fighting all my life simply disappears. I can concentrate on doing what I like best, writing well and telling interesting stories.'

'How have your books been received?'

'Often better than the books I published under my own name. That was a trick Greta Garbo taught me.'

'Did you know Garbo?'

'We were good friends. I had been called the Greta Garbo of literature so often that when we accidentally ran into each other on the corner of Second Avenue and 47th Street she came right over to me and introduced herself. As you can imagine I was beside myself with pride. She and Marilyn Monroe were my two best women friends in the movie industry.'

'My God, did you know Marilyn too?'

'Hey, take it easy there. Marilyn and I were friends all the way back in the 50s. We met in the waiting room of our mutual psychiatrist, a German woman who had been a patient of Freud's. We got to talking in the waiting room because we always arrived at the same time and our therapist was always delayed because of the patients before us.'

Salinger had a faraway look in his eyes. I let him alone, then I asked, 'Tell me how you write.'

'Every morning I go over to the little house I built on the grounds. I lie down on the sofa because of a back injury I've had since the war and write by hand. I write with the same pencils and on the same paper that Hemingway used. I met him during the war in France. I looked him up and asked him to read a short story I had written. When he'd read it he picked up a revolver and shot the head off a chicken to show his appreciation. Never was I given higher praise. We corresponded until just before he died. I went to his funeral in Ketchum, Idaho. Hemingway taught me a lot of things, the most important of which was to make sure you stop writing while there's still water in the well. But he also taught me a lot of technical tricks. Whenever he and William Faulkner were in New York we'd meet and get drunk. The only problem was that I can't hold my liquor and I invariably fell asleep out by the hatcheck and would miss the words of wisdom those two old drunks were spouting. Faulkner gave me his old typewriter before he died. The machine still has the little handwritten message he'd put on it. 'Kill your darlings,' it says. I try to but it's harder than you think. I use the machine to type up my handwritten manuscripts. Then Helen takes over on the computer. Helen is a retired Cornish school teacher who's typed things up for me for years.'

'Here comes the million dollar question that all your fans are dying to ask you. Why did you decide never to give a single interview?'

'I'll try to answer that as exhaustively as possible. First of all there was Kierkegaard, our mutual friend. He hid behind any number of pseudonyms. Kierkegaard was my hero, so the obvious thing to do was follow his example. It made me feel close to him. But there were a number of other things in my personal life that were decisive. Towards the end of the war in Europe I had a massive nervous breakdown. It was due partly to total exhaustion and partly to what I had witnessed. I was one of the first American soldiers to enter a liberated concentration camp and I saw what the Germans had done to my fellow Jews. My nervous system has never been the same since. Hence my radical decision to live in peace. The consequences that decision has had on my life were completely unpredictable. I feel like a criminal. My only crime is that I want to be left alone. They talk about me as if I was a madman, a saint or a fairly well functioning psychopath. It's been particularly hard on my family. For them it's almost like living with a wanted criminal. At the same time my decision not to give interviews has cemented my celebrity status. Very few people actually have any idea what I've written. To most people I'm known as the guy who doesn't give interviews or appear on TV. My celebrity is due solely to a polite but definite 'No thanks.' I'm a freak in a world where communications have gone haywire.'

'*Are* you a freak?'

'No, there's nothing mysterious about me. I'm a normal person, usually a very happy person. I love my work, my friends, my family. I enjoy excellent health. I've been a health freak all my life. I'm a self-taught herbalist, I can heal with herbs. I'm a completely average, banal old man.'

'Why do you say banal?'

'Because I'm completely uninteresting as a private individual. Marlon Brando has been a good friend of mine for years. As a private individual he's almost boring. Marlon came up here once with John Lennon and Bob Dylan, who wanted to meet me. We were four unusually boring men. What we really sounded like was a group of travelling salesmen talking shop.'

'Can I get you to talk about women?'

'Oh, please don't hold back! Just stick your nose right into my private life! I've always lived surrounded by women. I've been married twice, first time to a German woman right after the war and then to Claire, who's the mother of my two children. She lives in California now, my daughter lives there too. She's a psychotherapist, my son is an actor and film producer. Now I'm living with that wonderful woman you saw driving the car.'

'One of your girlfriends, Joyce Maynard, wrote a book about her affair with you when she was 18 and you were 55.'

'Yes.'

'Have you read it?'

'Of course.'

'What do you think of it?'

'Apart from the fact that I come across as a dirty old man forcing an innocent young girl to have oral sex with him, the book is quite well written.'

'They say you're attracted to very young women?'

'I'm attracted to young women and old women both. Woody Allen and I, we're old friends, are considering founding The Dirty Old Man's Club. Men with wives 40 years younger than themselves get to join free.'

'How did you meet Woody Allen?'

'The usual way. He wrote me many years ago. We're both in therapy so we exchange experiences. Woody gave me the name of a therapist who helped him for many years. He finally stopped going to him because the guy kept insisting he was an infantile narcissist. I was an extra in four of Woody's films. See if you can find me. Woody even made a movie about me. *Zelig* is about a man who only is what everybody else wants him to be. That's me. Or it *was* me. Maybe that's why I'm so dependent on women. I dry up and disappear if I'm not with a woman. I really am dependent on women on every level. Graham Greene used to say it came as a surprise to him that the dependency gets worse the older you get. He had always thought that desire would dull with age, but that's not how it is. You're in for a surprise if you're expecting a peaceful old age.'

'How did you meet Graham Greene?'

'He was a good friend of Georges Simenon whom I

met when he was living in America. All three of us used to meet at least once a year either in Antibes where Greene had an apartment in a building near the harbour or in Switzerland at Simenon's place. Sometimes Noel Coward joined us and one memorable evening we went over to visit Chaplin and Oona. Oona still made my heart beat faster. Noel Coward sang for us and Chaplin accompanied him on the piano, and Oona and I danced just like we used to at the Stork Club in New York before the war. So don't tell me I live an isolated life!'

'Did you discuss women with Greene and Simenon?'

'Greene's theory about himself and women was that he could only get a relationship to work if the woman was married to another man, preferably a friend of his. He himself was sure it was a kind of homosexuality in disguise, a way of being intimate with other men by sleeping with their wives. Simenon, on the other hand, made a big deal of having slept with ten thousand women. He told Federico Fellini while they were sitting under a big tree getting interviewed by some French magazine. Simenon thought all good writers hated their mothers, that's why they had become writers. He told me he had been sending money to his mother in Belgium for all those years. When she died they found all that money in a shoebox under her bed. It was her final rejection of him. She preferred his brother. That's what all his novels were about, he said.'

'What are your books about?'

'Read Kierkegaard, pal, and you'll find out.'

'Your daughter recently wrote a book about her life with you?'

'She did.'

'Have you read it?'

'Of course. I wasn't the easiest father to live with to put it mildly. But I'm an old man now. When I die the vultures will pounce the way they swooped on Greta Garbo when she died. So it's better my daughter writes something approaching the truth and actually makes some money on it. I love my daughter. It's only natural that her feelings towards me are more complex than mine are for her. When Marilyn Monroe came and stayed with us she always slept on a camp bed in my daughter's room. They'd lay there all night talking. I may have been impossible but I did have friends worth talking to.'

The interview terminated there. We had turned back towards Cornish for the last part. Salinger's wife pulled into the parking lot behind the supermarket where she had picked us up a little less than an hour ago. I could see my wife waiting with Art and Rose by the store entrance. I gave Salinger the folder containing his letters.

He shook my hand, I got out of the car, and as soon as the car door shut behind me, the woman accelerated and Salinger and his wife drove out of the parking lot. The last I saw of him he was taking off his glasses and cleaning them with a white handkerchief.

All the way back to New York and the following day I was in a daze. I had met my hero, the mythical Salinger, and it had been even better than I'd hoped.

The fairy tale ended abruptly when two women I'd never met knocked on our door at the Hotel Pioneer. They were young, both in their 30s, both dressed in black, both frighteningly efficient. They told us they represented one of the biggest law firms in New York.

They informed me in no uncertain terms that if I had any plans of publishing the Salinger interview they would sue the shit out of me, or words to that effect. The parties that were interested in acquiring the letters Salinger had written to me had been obliged to do a little number on me: When they had realised I wasn't going to sell the letters they had resorted to Plan B: The person I had interviewed was a fake. He wasn't Salinger but a Salinger lookalike, an out of work actor who had presented himself as Salinger. The most sensible thing for me to do was to return to Denmark and keep *very quiet*.

They left the hotel room without saying goodbye.

The next day we tried to get hold of Art and Rose but to no avail. None of the telephone numbers they had given us was answered. When we went to the lawyers' office on 57th Street where we'd had the meeting with them nobody had ever heard of Art or Rose.

The credit card we'd been given was closed of course. We tried to find out who had issued it but no one could say.

The story could have ended there. But it didn't.

Beate and I were walking down 6th Avenue after we had given up trying to reach Art and Rose. I was dazed, reeling from pure depression.

Beate was in excellent spirits. She said, 'We'll be hearing from them again.'

'From whom?'

'Art and Rose.'

'Why ?'

'We have something they want.'

'And what might that be?'

'A bunch of letters worth a fortune.'

'But I gave them to Salinger, the fake Salinger.'

'No you didn't.'

'What are you talking about? I gave them to him myself.'

'What you gave him were copies.'

'What are you talking about?'

'I had copies made of all the letters before we left.'

'That's a lie!'

'Dan, I'm a dentist. Some of the biggest crooks in Denmark are my patients. These are people who have embezzled billions. It was no problem getting them to advise me.'

'I can't believe what I'm hearing! Why didn't you tell me before?'

'I was nervous enough. I didn't want to spoil things for you.'

'Have you suspected them all along? Without telling me? You're treating me like a child!'

'Dan, the issue here is not whether or not you're a child. The point is I love you and it doesn't hurt to be careful, does it?'

'I'll never stop being a little kid lost in the woods, is that it?'

'Oh stop being so sorry for yourself. I can't stand listening to you.'

'Well, what happens now?'

'We'll be hearing from Salinger and his gang, I warrant.'

'Where are the letters?'

'That's something I'm not going to tell even you', she laughed.

We continued down 6th Avenue and I felt as if I was being sucked straight into a black hole.

Whenever depression strikes and I'm groping around in the dark for help, one person stands out: Ib Schroder, my deceased father-in-law, the orthognathic surgeon, the children's grandfather, Salinger's Danish friend.

Everything important about depression I learned from him.

'Give it a face, make it concrete,' he would say. 'Depression is a nebulous, amorphous mental process. It tends to lift when you grab hold of it.'

Make it concrete, give it names, faces. Depression isn't just depression. Visualize it. A depression is always people, faces.

I gave it faces. First, Ib Schroder's face. Behind his face was Kierkegaard's. Behind his was Salinger's.

Salinger's face. The fake Salinger. Salinger hiding behind someone paid to play the role of Salinger. Maybe the real Salinger doesn't exist. Maybe he never existed.

97

Maybe he's an artificial product, an author right out of Andy Warhol's philosophy of art. A machine. A sphinx. A mirror. You think you're looking Salinger in the face but all you see is yourself in a mirror. You only see what you want to see. You see only yourself.

I had travelled all this way to meet Salinger only to encounter myself. Concrete enough for you, Ib? Now what?

Ib's counsel came promptly. 'Keep moving. Stay on the path. You're on an endless journey into the darkness within you. Seek out those friends who can help you.'

Help me do what? I had barely formulated the question when the answer came to me.

The answer is eyes. The answer has *always* been eyes.

I looked into Beate's eyes. It's ok to look into your wife's eyes. In Beate's eyes I saw what I had to do here in New York.

Beate is the only woman I ever loved and who ever loved me. If I hadn't had the extraordinary good luck to meet her I would never have experienced love. I would probably be dead in fact. It's as simple as that, as complicated as that, it's the truth. She knows it and I know it. There's no need to say it aloud.

I am not a marketable commodity. No one with depression is. Beate is a marketable commodity, without her I'm nothing. When something happens to me it doesn't seem real until I've told her. I can't experience anything myself, I can't enjoy anything myself. I don't have eyes.

All my life I've wanted eyes of my own.

I've used other people's eyes. I know how Kierkegaard sees the world, I perceive the world through his eyes. I know Salinger's eyes, I enter his universe and look through *his* eyes.

Who can help me find my own eyes? I decided *now* was the time, here in New York.

I had resolved any number of times before this that *now* was the time, but nothing had happened.

Why should anything be any different now?

There was no answer to that.

Seek out the friends who can help you.

It's in your head. Anything can happen.

I took the train out to the Bronx Botanical Gardens and stayed there for hours until it got dark, journeying back to the friends Ib spoke of, dead and alive.

NINE

The Journey Back Into the Dark Woods to Seek Advice

Naturally it was Puk who helped me get the best anti-depressant advice I ever had. She always knows somebody. If there's someone she doesn't know, she always knows someone who can put her in touch with the right person.

For Puk it was a challenge to ferret out the top Kierkegaard experts and establish connections. If all else failed she'd call the head of the Kierkegaard research centre and say the magic words, 'Hello, Puk Bonnesen speaking.'

Her name is the *open sesame* that opens all doors. Puk unearthed the name of the person who knew most about Kierkegaard's little sentence on the sympathetic and the antipathetic that I had spent so much time studying, an 87-year-old former pastor and associate professor at Århus University, Else Marie Vandborg. Almost blind and living in a nursing home in Frederiksberg, she was a Doctor of Theology and her doctor's thesis dealt with the concept of love in Kierkegaard.

Two of her grandchildren met me in front of the nursing home one Tuesday morning. Else Marie Vandborg was standing by the window in her room when we knocked on the door. She was a tall woman with white hair, and her dark eyes peered out at me with the look of the visually impaired. The two grandchildren had arranged it so that she and I should sit next to each other on a sofa against the wall next to the window. It was very quiet. Tea and cookies were produced.

We sat down and the grandchildren left.

'Let's call each other by our first names, shall we?' was the first thing she said.

'With pleasure. My name is Dan.'

Her voice was high-pitched and clear and she talked very loud. She said, 'Puk Bonnesen told me you're a descendant of Poul Martin Moller. Is that true?'

'No, it isn't true.'

She laughed. 'Nevertheless, it's a sympathetic thought. Moller was such a sympathetic man. I was so busy studying Kierkegaard all my life that I came to feel we were close relatives. My Uncle Soren, my devoted Soren Kierkegaard, with whom I've shared so many joys.'

'To be honest I feel related to Poul Martin Moller, too. I often read him when I'm in need of comfort.'

'My grandchild tells me you suffer from melancholy.'

'Yes, that's correct.'

'Tell me, Dan, why do you want to talk to me?'

I told her about Salinger and the correspondence.

She listened and then asked. 'Have you come because of Salinger or for yourself?'

'Both.'

'What do you want to know?'

'What does Kierkegaard mean by the sympathetic and the antipathetic?'

Else Marie bent forward groping for the tea thermos. She rattled the tea cup. I reached out to help her but she pushed away my hand saying, 'Thank you, young Moller, but I can manage.'

She insisted on pouring the tea and spilled some on the table.

Then she offered me a cookie. 'Coconut macaroons baked by my youngest grandchild, a boy. I would so much have liked for him to be named Soren, but they called him William. And it *is* the right name for him.'

We spoke of Puk Bonnesen and Nora From, both of whom she had read. Her son had read Boris Schauman aloud to her. She said, 'Schauman is always flexing his verbal muscles, which I find extremely tiresome. What about yourself, Dan. Are you a great writer or a little writer?'

'I'm a little writer.'

'Some people prefer little writers. I know I do.'

'That's very kind of you, Else Marie.'

'I won't tell you whether I've read your work until you tell me if you've read my Kierkegaard dissertation.'

'No, I haven't.'

'Well, I haven't read your work either!' she said and gave a loud laugh.

We spoke of Kierkegaard's death in the hospital on Bredegade and the family dispute that prevented a headstone from being erected on his grave for so long.

'Well, my little poet,' she said. 'Maybe we should talk about what you came to hear. One little sentence by Kierkegaard.'

'Puk tells me you're the expert.'

'Puk Bonnesen is a born flatterer.'

'But she's right, isn't she?'

Else Marie smiled and nodded. 'Well, at any rate I'm the person who's devoted most time to that sentence. My father was melancholic and his father before him. I know what it's like growing up in a melancholy family.'

'What is your own temperament like?'

'I've woken up in excellent spirits almost every morning of my life.'

'I could tell by reading your dissertation.'

'So you *did* read it? I thought you said you hadn't.'

'I lied.'

'Why did you do that?'

'I was afraid you'd start examining me on it. They say you were merciless, brutal in fact, at the oral exams.'

'Little poet, you're flattering me and caning me at the same time.'

'I'm sorry.'

'Well, I'm going to give you an exam anyway. You say you can tell I have a cheerful temperament by reading my dissertation. Would you care to exemplify?'

'Remember the part about Parnassus, the exalted cultural circle that everyone wanted to be part of, the Heiberg family's intellectual salon at Sokvæsthus in

Christianshavn? You describe how Kierkegaard and Hans Christian Andersen were allowed in a couple of times even though everyone made fun of the two insecure, gauche, young men behind their backs?'

'Yes indeed, page 275,' said Else Marie. 'What's so remarkable about that?'

'What comes next? You write unexpectedly: "If anyone had whispered to the cultural elite snickering behind their hands in the salon in Christianshavn that the only reason they would be remembered today is precisely because of those two gauche young men, they would have thought it a bad joke."'

'Heavens! You remember the exact wording on the bottom of page 275!'

'So do you, Else Marie.'

'Certainly, but I wrote it!'

'I don't remember a single word I ever wrote myself.'

'Little poet, that's obvious in your work.'

'So you *have* read my work.'

'Dan, what do you take me for? Here's a young writer who leaves no stone unturned in trying to talk to me. Don't you think I was just a little curious to find out who he is, what sort of thing he writes and why he might be interested in talking to me?'

'Did you find out?'

'Very likely. Let's put it to the test.'

Else Marie picked up a bag made of some kind of fabric from the floor next to her chair. In the bag were some papers and a large magnifying glass. She brought the magnifying glass to her eye and looked at me through it.

'Young Moller, I may be the only person in the world who's read your texts under a magnifying glass.'

'What was the result?'

'There goes your author's ego sitting up, wagging its tail, and begging to be scratched behind the ears!'

'Hey, that's a line straight out of Puk Bonnesen.'

'Exactly, but who do you think she stole it from?'

'You?'

'Precisely. I said it once on a radio program.'

'Puk steals anything she can get her hands on.'

'You wouldn't be here without her, little poet.'

'I'd be dead without her,' I said. 'Sorry. It wasn't my intention to go on about myself. Please forgive me.'

'Dan, I've made inquiries about you. You have a reason for reading that Kierkegaard sentence under a magnifying glass. Kierkegaard wrote it for people like you. You were depressed and suicidal as a child. I know that. That's why I agreed to see you today.'

'Thank you.'

'Furthermore, you're quite a good-looking young fellow who flatters me to just the right extent. I would probably have agreed to see you even if you weren't suicidal.'

'Can you actually see me?'

'Not very clearly, but I've studied photos of you under the magnifying glass. You're definitely on the good-looking side, but you look arrogant and withdrawn, almost hostile.'

'Sounds like me alright.'

'What do you think of the way I look?'

'Else Marie if you want to hear the truth from an arrogant, hostile writer, I have looked at photos of you when you were young under a magnifying glass. You're beautiful now that you're old. But you must have been *sensational* when you were young. Rumour has it that Georg Brandes was madly in love with you.'

'Brandes spoke to me of the times he'd met Hans Christian Andersen, his left hand resting absentmindedly on my knee all the while.'

'That gives us a direct connection back to Kierkegaard through Brandes and Andersen.'

Else Marie said, 'Ah, Kierkegaard was always my contemporary. My love for him is purely physical. I've spent more hours with him than with anyone else. It's as though everything he wrote was written directly to me. I can feel his body heat, his breathing.'

'I feel the same way. I just don't completely understand what he writes. That's why I've taken the liberty of intruding on you, Else Marie.'

'Well, you've come to the right person, Dan. I believe I'm the only one who really understands what Kierkegaard means when he speaks of sympathetic antipathy and antipathetic sympathy.'

'What does he mean then?'

Else Marie picked up the magnifying glass again. But instead of holding it over the papers on the table in front of her, she held it to my eyes. I looked into her eyes, several times magnified.

She began to explain. 'The key concept for Kierkegaard is guilt. This is the origin of all the misinterpretations. It's Kierkegaard's own fault. He writes about guilt; we all owe a debt, he says. Most people think he's talking about sin, that we're born sinners due to original sin. This is a mistake. Kierkegaard means something completely different when he speaks of guilt. Guilt is a good thing. Guilt is a positive thing. Do you follow me, Dan?'

'No, to be honest, I don't think I do.'

'Guilt is an optimistic, edifying term in Kierkegaard. That's my thesis. Guilt should not be understood the way we do today in the sense that you're guilty, you've committed a crime, you're a born criminal or anything like that. No. That's not what he meant. Guilt should be understood as the opposite of innocence. What Kierkegaard is saying is that you should *never* be innocent. You should *never* be the innocent victim things happen to. No matter whether you're knocked down on the street or run over or struck by lightning, you're *always* in some way responsible. *Never* be the innocent victim. Why not? Because if you're innocent, you have no options. Even if you really are completely innocent of something that happens, then against all logic you must insist that you are *not* innocent. On a certain level you're always responsible for what happens to you. You're guilty. Only when you're guilty, the opposite of innocent, that is, can you act. Do you understand, little poet?'

'Yes.'

'If you just stand there like a chump waiting for disaster to strike, you're innocent. Go forward, go sideways, just go, move. Where should you go? What compass should you follow? The compass is contained in Kirekegaard's sentence: Go where the sympathetic collides with the antipathetic. If you hold back, you'll always be on the outside looking in; you'll always be an innocent child. It's very pleasant being an innocent child. It's secure. Your surroundings like you when you're an innocent child and that makes you feel sheltered. You encounter no hostility, but being an innocent child causes anxiety and depression. If you want to overcome that anxiety you have to engage in the struggle between the sympathetic and the antipathetic. It hurts, but that's the arena where the battle against melancholy is fought. That's where you must go!'

TEN

Two Stars in a Car

When people like me it's because I'm an intimate of Puk, Boris and Nora and work with them. People never come right out and say so, but it's always there. They find it strange that I'm the Factory's fourth member.

What do the three others see in me? they wonder. I must have hidden qualities invisible to the uninitiated.

Most people are cautious about approaching the three others through me. People usually only approach me when a friendship is at stake. It's not unusual for Boris to break off a friendship, form a new one and then pick up the old one again and start all over. Boris quickly becomes enthusiastic but his enthusiasm cools just as quickly. His friends and ex-friends are well aware that it's no use coming to me to mend a broken friendship.

It's different with Puk and Nora. They don't break off friendships. They do something even crueler, they downgrade them. This occurs gradually and almost imperceptibly at first. A promised phone call isn't made. The tone is slightly cooler when you meet on the street or at a party. There's nothing to put your finger on, it's merely a touch, a vague disquiet. The light of the friendship slowly goes out. Finally there's that dinner party you would normally have been invited to but the invitation never arrives.

Of course, you don't just call and say, 'Hey, what's wrong? I'm always invited to your Sunday morning get-togethers in August. What am I missing here?'

No, they come to me, Dan Moller, instead. I'm less dangerous to approach. They think up some kind of pretext. Slowly they work the conversation around to what they really called about. How is Puk these days, or Nora? What's going on in their lives that made them change their routines? Do I know something they don't?

As Puk would put it: My power to appeal lies not in myself but in the reflected glory of others. I never tried to intervene on anyone's behalf. I knew that could get me in trouble, especially when it came to Puk's circle of friends. Nora's circle got together to have fun. They weren't interested in power or cultural status. But it was different with Puk, which was why I normally wouldn't dream of getting mixed up in what was going on.

There was the classic Puk situation: People thought they were her friends, that she liked them, they were in her confidence. Suddenly they found themselves off the best friends list with not a word of explanation.

At one point I was working at a TV studio out in Gladsaxe. I took the bus back and forth. One afternoon when I was on my way to the bus stop, a car pulled up. A woman rolled down the window and asked if I wanted a lift back to town.

I knew her face and the face of the man sitting next to

her. I had never spoken to them before. In my opinion they were Denmark's greatest movie stars, the ultimate when it came to talent, charm and star quality. They were the couple Lise Ringheim and Henning Moritzen.

I got into the backseat of their car. I was a devoted fan meeting my adored idols, and here they were talking to me as though we were old friends. We were soon calling each other Dan, Lise and Henning. I was in seventh heaven.

I felt like opening the window and calling out to the world at large: 'Hey, do you realise who this is! I'm in Moritzen's and Ringheim's back seat! They're talking to me! Call my mother and father and sisters and brothers and tell them I just met Lise and Henning. I'm in their car!'

It took me back to when I was a kid and the walls of my room were plastered with posters of movie stars. Two of those posters had just opened up and let me in. Lise and Henning. I repeated their names to myself. It was almost too unbelievable to be true.

I felt I knew everything about them. I would never be able to choose between them; they were a couple. But if I did have to choose I would choose Lise Ringheim. As an actress as well as a private individual she was in a class by herself, in my opinion.

I was struck dumb with awe at the situation. I wasn't too dazzled though, not to be fully aware there was a reason for all this and the reason lay with the three others at the Factory. I didn't care. Here I was and they were talking to me as though we were old friends.

111

Puk had already pointed out my tendency to prostrate myself before people I proclaimed unique and therefore worshipped like a teenager. She discussed this in an article on idol worship but I felt it was addressed directly to me. Puk's point was that idol worship is a kind of suicide in disguise. Instead of physically killing yourself you get rid of yourself by moving entirely into someone else's universe.

You can never be entirely sure whether Puk is joking or not. That's part of her attraction and it keeps people on their toes. You'd rather laugh once too often than once too little with Puk.

I had been in the back seat for just a few minutes when something happened that suddenly changed the entire situation.

Lise Ringheim was driving so I could see her eyes in the rear view mirror. She was wearing sun glasses but she took them off. Our eyes met, and I immediately under-stood she was suffering from the same thing I was. She was depressed. She hid it very well, but one depressed person can spot another a long way off.

She nodded to me. She'd seen the expression in my eyes, too. She said, 'Henning and I were good friends of Ib Schroder's. We often met him at Mogens Fog's.'

Mortizen and Ringheim had treated me all along as though we were old friends. Suddenly I felt it was true. They had known my father-in-law. They knew a lot about me.

Henning glanced at Lise who nodded. Then he told me

about their little problem, as he called it. They had been friends of Puk Bonnesen for some time. Now she had become reserved towards them. Not only that, Puk was the gateway to a lot of other people they really wanted to keep in touch with.

This was a serious problem for them, I felt. Nevertheless it was the funniest thing I'd heard for ages. It put me in a good mood.

I had no idea why it should cheer me up so much. The situation simply served as a powerful anti-depressant.

'I'll take care of it,' I said without having the slightest idea how I'd go about it.

Lise said bleakly, 'Dan, you call the shots.'

Henning turned around and looked at me as if to make sure I'd understood what Lise had said.

He patted my knee and smiled. 'Maybe you think you know a lot about us, but I can assure you we know ten times more about you.'

He turned around and looked out the windshield again.

Just before Lyngby, Lise passed a truck at high speed. She looked at me at regular intervals in the rear view mirror and explained:

'For many years we've been part of a circle of intellectuals. They're the only people we can be ourselves with. They like us for what we are and not for what we do. Do you understand? It would be a minor disaster if they drop us. It would almost be like dying.'

Henning said. 'What do you mean, minor disaster? It would be a *major* disaster.'

113

'Do you understand what we're saying?' asked Lise.

'Yes,' I replied. 'But I just have to get used to the fact I'm in Mortizen's and Ringheim's back seat, talking to them as if we've known each other forever.'

Henning turned around and smiled. 'We've known you a long time because we realise our lives are in your hands, if you'll pardon the somewhat melodramatic turn of phrase. You're the star here, Dan. You're the one in control.'

Lise said, 'It may sound like an exaggeration, Dan, but Henning's right. We've been planning how to run into you by chance for a long time.'

Henning smiled broadly and said. 'We've studied you so carefully we feel sure you understand what we mean.'

Henning was a master of imitation, I knew. The person he was imitating now was me. He had my dry, slightly didactic way of talking down pat.

He smiled delightedly when I cracked up. Tears came out of my eyes and snot out of my nose. Henning knew I thought he was the funniest man in the world, and he enjoyed it.

He also knew that I knew that his charm offensive was well prepared. Now that I was reduced to a cackling hen he proceeded to his next number.

'Of course I enjoy your finding me funny. But at the same time I *hate* you. You think I call the shots, but you do. All you have to do is stop laughing and in a second I'm reduced to looking like a manipulative asshole.'

Henning had kept up his imitation of my pedantic

way of talking. He had me in the palm of his hand and proceeded with what he had rehearsed.

'Every evening when we're scheduled to perform at the theatre we go onto the stage in plenty of time before the audience arrives. We go all the way out to the edge of the stage and look down at the empty seats. And we say, 'Fuck you, you predators! Go home to wherever you come from, your stupid little row houses. Put a bullet through your brains. Put your heads in a gas oven. Find something better to do than coming here and turning thumbs up or thumbs down.' Then we go up to our dressing rooms, our peace of mind restored, ready to go down to the stage again and satisfy the many-headed monster in the house.'

Henning waited until I had dried my eyes and then he delivered the coup de grace. 'Fuck you, Dan Thorvald Moller. You and your left wing, radical chic, wine-guzzling pals. Our lives are in your hands. We're in free fall out here and the only one that can bring us down to earth alive is you. You're a monster! *You* call the shots!'

I doubled over in the back seat, and felt the wind had been knocked right out of me.

ELEVEN

At a Nursing Home in Frederiksberg

Kierkegaard wrote: 'Life can only be understood backwards, but it must be lived forwards.' Else Marie Vandborg and I agreed this was only moderately true. I understood my life better after I had met her; I incorporated her into the life I was living forwards. Meeting her was the turning point of my life. She was with me every day in everything I did. Else Marie Vandborg was one of the most powerfully antidepressant human beings I'd ever met.

She fell one morning in her room at the nursing home and broke her hip. I visited her once at the hospital and another time when she was back in the nursing home in Frederiksberg.

I felt about her the way I felt about Nora. The mere fact that here was someone I could tell anything meant I didn't have to seek her out.

She was my direct link to Kierkegaard. She knew Kierkegaard had been my salvation and she herself was the mainstay of my life.

She always laughed when I told her that.

'I can barely keep alive myself and there you go making me out to be some kind of lifeline in a troubled sea.'

'That's what you are to me,' I said.

'Dear little poet, it would be more accurate to say you're *my* lifeline. My children and grandchildren are kind, they visit me, but they find it harder and harder to know what to talk to me about. With you I can talk for hours because we have Kierkegaard in common.'

In our minds' eyes we strolled through the Latin quarter of Copenhagen near the University. We attended lectures with Kierkegaard, we listened to Sibbern lecture and especially Poul Martin Moller lecturing on the Greek philosophers. We imagined the two men, Kierkegaard and Moller, meeting after the lecture. Kierkegaard was a great admirer of Moller. Moller was almost a father to him. Kierkegaard felt safe in the older man's company. They would talk for hours in a coffee house on Nytorv square.

Our common interest in a single sentence by Kierkegaard furnished us with material for endless discussions. When we met we first caught up on her health and whatever minor matters I could help her with. I showed her photos of Beate and our two daughters. Then we turned to what really interested us. We plunged into the sentence. Down in the sentence there was always plenty of space and elbow room for both of us, for hours on end.

Else Marie said: 'You could spend your entire life in just one of those words, isn't that true, Dan? Is it sympathy or antipathy you'd rather be in?

'How do you know everything about me?' I asked.

She put her hand on my arm and laughed. 'Dear, sweet little poet. All it takes is just a few minutes with you to be able to see deep into your soul.'

'Even if you're blind?'

'Especially if you're blind. Almost blind.'

'Else Marie, no one has ever said such things to me before.'

That made her laugh even louder. 'Now don't go getting any ideas into your head, little writer. What you want is what we all want. We're all lost without it. It's what our friend wrote about all the time.'

'And there I was thinking I was special.'

'It's all right there in our sentence! Clear as day. Study the word sympathy and what do you find? Everything your heart is full of.'

Together Else Marie and I descended into our chosen sentence. We found ourselves inside the word sympathy. We explored it that first day and all the following days I visited her at the nursing home.

That afternoon in the nursing home when Else Marie and I descended together into the word sympathy for the first time, I felt I had come home. I had reached the haven I had been seeking. All my life I'd hoped to find a place I could call home. For the most part it was an aimless journey in the dark, driven by hunches, intuition. The journey for all its mistakes had been necessary; it couldn't have been any shorter. I was young and depressed, and there was no way anyone was going to hand me a user's guide to a Kierkegaard sentence that

118

said: Go down into the word sympathy, that's where you belong, that's your home, that's where you'll find the answer to all your questions. In the word 'sympathy'.

Else Marie was probably the only person who had delved into the concept so deeply. She understood it backwards and forwards. She felt secure down there and had no trouble showing me around. It was her contention, and Kierkegaard's, that all human beings could feel at home in that sentence and in that word.

As a child the word sympathy repelled me; being depressed I was well aware there was no getting around it. When I started studying the Salinger Syndrome I had to find words for everything the term sympathy encompassed. I found it humiliating to articulate my deepest needs, but I knew I needed to find the right words. Without words everything would simply remain an amorphous mass of emotions and desires. Ib Schroder, my father-in-law, made me put my desires into words. The words were then and are now: friendship, attention, and love.

These are three basic necessities. To get them you need to have a well running how-to-please mechanism. My how-to-please mechanism, or enzyme as I called it, didn't work. It was off balance. I had spent half my depressed life studying that imbalance. When I met Else Marie Vandborg certain things started to fall into place. I could say the words friendship, attention and love aloud without feeling embarrassed or ashamed.

Else Marie said, 'I wish I could live for another couple

of years, Dan. We could explore your three words in depth together. Kierkegaard would be pleased with us. I'll soon be twice his age when he died but there's still not enough time.'

Else Marie got seven more months. She died one winter night. She left me a small collection of books and a long handwritten letter that I still read on the evening of the last Friday of every month. Always in the evening so there's a chance Else Marie will show up in my dreams.

TWELVE

A Fairy Tale in the Botanical Gardens

We all knew Puk knew Frederik Dessau. When Puk said, 'Frederik told me', we knew it wasn't just any old Frederik, it was Frederik Dessau.

There was no need to brief us on him (b 1927; Sweden, during the war: alone at school in Lund. Currently a ubiquitous member of the Danish literary scene: author, journalist, director, own radio program, etc.)

Puk gave us to understand that Frederik knew everyone worth knowing.

According to Puk, Danish cultural life is composed of five circles. Within the confines of these five worlds, these five universes, all the right people are to be found. If you belong to one circle you have a minimum of professional contact with members of any of the other circles, and no private contact whatsoever.

According to Puk Frederik Dessau was one of the few individuals who moved freely among all the circles. He had his own circle, of course, but no social sanctions were ever imposed if he ventured out of it.

When Puk quoted Frederik, the rest of us listened. When Puk quoted Frederik on friendship I was particularly attentive. Needless to say Puk was quoting Frederik

121

here: 'Frederik says that friendships are lifelong and unconditional. They're not up for discussion. If they are, then they're not friendships.'

Boris' comment was: 'Then I have no friends and never have. Hasn't Frederik ever given a friend a good kick in the ass? Hasn't he ever been green with envy over a friend's success?'

'I asked him that,' Puk responded. 'The answer is no. You want only the best for your friends.'

Boris nodded. 'Can I get to meet him?'

Puk shook her head. 'He refuses to meet you three. He says all three of you are cannibals. You'd chew him up and eat him alive and put him in one of your stories using his real name. He thinks you'd do better to use your poetic imagination inventing fictional characters.'

A few months later I happened to be walking behind Puk and Frederik on Blegdamsvej in Osterbro late one afternoon. We were aware they met regularly and went for a walk. I was shamelessly envious of both of them. I felt left out. I was dying to hear a word-for-word account of what they were saying. Vindictively I muttered, 'I'm going to get you, Frederik. Moller the Cannibal is going to turn you into the character in a novel under your own name. And there's nothing you can do about it, no matter how much you protest.'

'Frederik Dessau was walking down Blegdamsvej in Osterbro one afternoon in October. . It was drizzling.'

Regardless of his wishes Frederik Dessau became a character in a novel.

To the rest of us Frederik came to symbolise all the people Puk knew and insisted on keeping to herself.

Nora began to speak of 'a Frederik'. She felt the best novel of the year should be awarded a small statue of Frederik Dessau. 'Who's going to get this year's Frederik, I wonder?' she asked.

Let others have their Nobels, their Oscars, their Bodils. At the Factory we dreamed solely of winning a Frederik.

We all knew that the real life Frederik was friends with Leif Panduro, the writer.

All writers have their dreams and fantasies. One of mine was that the telephone would ring one day and a voice would say: 'Hi Dan, this is Leif Panduro. I'd love to get to know you. When can we meet?'

Leif Panduro was far and away Denmark's most popular author. His novels were read avidly, his television plays were national events. Whenever a new television play by Leif Panduro was on, the streets were empty.

His life was well known. It was the story of the dentist who became a novelist. It was the story of the wildly successful novel, *Rend mig i traditionerne*, 'Kick me in the Traditions'. He was called the conscience of Denmark, the mirror of his times.

I was often asked if I knew him, if I'd met him, the original writing dentist. Sadly, the answer was always no.

Then one evening there was a telephone call, or rather two telephone calls. At that time there was a huge ad plastered on the sides of all the Copenhagen buses saying

LEIF LOVES ESTHER. It was an ad for a weekly magazine in which Lise Norgaard interviewed Leif Panduro about his views on love. Everyone knew Esther was Leif Panduro's wife, also a dentist.

The first phone call was from Frederik Dessau. He was sorry to bother me, he said, he was calling for a good friend of his, Leif Panduro. Panduro was too nervous to call himself. He wanted to know if he could meet me as we were both dentists. Panduro had a few things he wanted to talk to me about. If I gave Frederik the green light he'd call Panduro, who would then call me.

Of course I gave the green light. I waited by the phone. Shortly afterwards I heard a voice I already knew so well from countless television programs. 'Dan Moller? Please forgive me for bothering you like this. It was just a sudden idea, understand? But Frederik said it was ok.'

We arranged to meet the next day at noon in the Botanical Gardens.

My first reaction was the wild desire to call the three others immediately and tell them what had happened.

My second reaction was imagining how in a few days I would casually mention, 'Oh, Leif told me.'

'Leif who?' one of the others would ask.

'Oh, Leif Panduro.'

'You know Leif Panduro?' 'Why didn't you say so?'

'I thought I had.'

'Do you know him *personally*?'

'We speak.'

'About what? Where? Do tell!'

124

The next day I was at the appointed place in the Botanical Gardens when I heard footsteps behind me. He must have been waiting for me behind a tree.

There he was, the celebrated Panduro; I knew just about everything about him, I believed. It was autumn Fall and the air was chilly. We could see our breath. He was wearing a green coat and a brown chequered scarf. He was slightly shorter than I had imagined. He was wearing glasses and had shaved off his moustache. Otherwise he was exactly as I had imagined.

We shook hands and exchanged courtesies.

I had read so much about his neuroses and phobias that I had a pretty good idea what he must be feeling. He didn't know me, I was a generation younger. It wasn't an ideal situation for him.

I suggested we take a walk around the Botanical Gardens. That way we could keep warm and take the edge off our nervousness.

We were suddenly in Panduro's world, two characters out of a television play by Leif Panduro. Two members of the bourgeoisie, the dying beast of prey, as he called it.

We talked about dentists. He had known my father-in-law. He had studied corrective jaw surgery with him. He had known him during the war and also knew he suffered from depression and had committed suicide.

He knew all about the Factory, too. What happened next is what usually happens whenever I meet other writers: they want to hear about the Factory, and particularly Puk Bonnesen.

However, Panduro wasn't merely curious. There was something troubling him.

'Whenever I have a television play going, Puk Bonnesen reviews it in *Information*. She's always very positive, but every single time she says my view on women is outdated.'

Was that why Panduro wanted to meet me? To get to Puk? To find out what Puk really thought about his view on women? Yes, indeed.

'It's really getting to me,' he said. 'Everything seems to revolve now around my outdated view on women.'

We walked on in silence. I had no opinion about Leif Panduro's view on women, and he had definitely not come to hear mine. Apart from the fact that I had no view on women.

We spoke of women. He told me about Esther and I told him about Beate.

He said, 'I hope you don't mind but I've picked up all kinds of information about you, to take the edge off my nervousness.'

'I have no secrets. You can ask me anything.'

'I've read some of what you've written. They say it's very autobiographical.'

'Well, it's what comes out of my head anyway.'

'May I call you Dan?'

'Of course, that's my name.'

'Puk Bonnesen always calls you Moller.'

'Oh, so you know that too?'

'Puk Bonnesen is one scary lady. I would never have the guts to meet her in person.'

'Panduro, you have no greater admirer than Puk.'

'Yes, that's what upsets me so much! Why does she think my view on women is outdated?'

'Maybe to make herself interesting. To attract your attention in the midst of all those glowing reviews?'

'Why should she want my attention?'

'I think she's in love with you. She thinks you're a sexy writer.'

'*Me* sexy? Are you having me on? I'm a sexual disaster. I'm about as sexy as a piece of soap.'

'Puk is extremely hygienic. I really don't think she finds soap unsexy.'

'Dan, you're sending on a wavelength I'm not picking up. You make me feel old. Just like my view on women. Ready for the grave.'

'Panduro, I'm really sorry. I'm your greatest fan. Even though I don't know you and have no wish to be intrusive I feel something like devotion towards you.'

'But you don't know me at all!'

'No, but that's just how it is.'

'Why don't you call me Leif?'

'There's nothing I'd like better.'

A woman was walking towards us on the path. She stopped.

'Aren't you Panduro? Leif Panduro?'

He smiled and tried to walk around her. 'Yes, I'm Panduro.'

The woman walked straight up to him. For a minute it looked as though she was going to embrace him, but

Panduro managed to dodge the embrace by taking a quick step backwards.

'I love you, Panduro!' she exclaimed.

'Thank you,' he said, and looked as though he'd been punched in the face.

'Your television play saved my life.'

'Oh, surely a slight exaggeration.'

'Your view of humanity, your human understanding. Your humanity makes me proud to be a Dane.'

'Does it?' asked Panduro, and looked as though he was about to cry.

'Shall I tell you what I said to my husband last night. About *you* , Leif Panduro, about *you*?'

I stepped in between Panduro and the woman and said, 'Please excuse us, madam, Leif Panduro has a dentist's appointment in a few minutes. He's suffering from a violent toothache. Unfortunately we must cut short this extremely interesting conversation.'

I led Panduro off down the path. He smiled apologetically to the woman, deeply regretting that he couldn't speak.

She called after us: 'The dentist has to go to the dentist! That's funny! It's just like a short story by Panduro!'

Panduro turned around and smiled weakly.

The woman followed us but stopped when she saw the expression on my face. I was making signs that Panduro was in great pain.

We hurried off. The next time someone crossed our path Panduro held his arm in front of his face to make sure he wasn't recognised.

'I've committed suicide,' he said. 'I no longer exist. I've become a tree in the Botanical Gardens that anyone can piss on.'

'Leif, I won't pretend to be stupider than I really am. I believe I completely understand what you're saying.'

'I know. That's why I came to you.'

'What do you want to know?'

'I know you are in correspondence with J.D. Salinger and you're working on formulating a theory called the Salinger Syndrome.'

'Who told you that?'

'Dan, you know in our milieu everyone talks to and about everyone else. That's how we make a living.'

'Tell me what you heard and who you heard it from.'

'I can't reveal my source, you know that. Otherwise it would dry up. The well would dry out.'

'What does your source say?'

'That you're working on a treatment for the Salinger Syndrome.'

'That's true, I am.'

'That you find most of your material in Kierkegaard.'

'That's true, too.'

'That you call it the Kierkegaard Cure.'

'Yes, that's pretty much it.'

'Is it a secret?'

'I've never really thought about it.'

'Is it a secret you suffer from depressions just like your father-in-law?'

'Leif, it simply never occurred to me anyone else could be interested.'

'You're a writer, Dan. You write about what interests you, about what's going on inside you. That's where your material comes from.'

'Yes, of course. Leif, I have no secrets from you. Your own work is an open book that anyone is free to read.'

'Can you help me Dan?'

'Is that why you're here?'

'Yes, I came to find out if you've found anything in the Kierkegaard Cure that could help me.'

'Are you depressed?'

'No, confused, terrified, appalled. I wanted success and it's boomeranged on me. I can't figure out how to tackle it. Leif, the private individual, has ceased to exist. I've committed suicide. And at the same time fame is a kind of drug, I need my daily fix. If I open the paper two days in a row and there's nothing about me I'm miserable. But at the same time all I want is for the writer Leif Panduro to disappear from the face of the earth so I no longer need to subject myself to people staring at me in the street. You know the worst part? It's when people write me and tell me their problems. They ask *me* for advice. Me. I don't even know how to keep from ruining my own life and my family's.'

'Welcome to the Salinger Syndrome,' I said.

'Can you help me?'

'I don't know. Give me a little time. A couple of minutes. Let's keep quiet and enjoy the plants and flowers.'

'My lips are sealed for the duration,' sighed Leif Panduro.

We looked at plants and flowers and bushes and trees. All the while I was thinking, 'There goes Dan Moller taking a walk in the Botanical Gardens with Leif Panduro. Dan and Leif. Leif and Dan. Tomorrow I'll be able to talk about him and everything we discussed.' This was apparently what I wanted more than anything else. To be able to say, 'Leif and I discussed this.'

It was childish, it was embarrassing; it was his problem in a nutshell. Even well educated adults went slightly berserk when they were in the presence of Leif Panduro.

Everything in the Botanical Gardens was surrounded by a special glow as we wandered around in silence reading the plant labels. I had Panduro's full attention because he was waiting for my answer. I gave myself plenty of time. He knew as well as I did I had no idea how to help him.

He said, 'Rumour has it that you're the only Danish writer that likes bad reviews. Is that true, Dan?'

'Yes, that's true.'

'Want to know how I feel about reviews? My wife reads them aloud to me. She reads them at night when we're in bed. When we've drawn the curtains and it's dark outside. She reads them aloud and makes comments. 'Is that really what they say about Panduro?' she says.'

'You've never read a review yourself?'

'Never! I'm much too self-centred!'

'You only get good reviews.'

131

'Yes, except for the ones that mention my antiquated view on women.'

'What does Esther say about that?'

'Esther? You know Esther?'

'Leif, LEIF LOVES ESTHER is written in capital letters on all the buses. Everybody knows your wife's name. Esther is as well known as a soccer player or a rock star.'

He stood stock still on the path and took hold of both my hands. 'Esther, for Chrissake! Esther has the answer to my problems! Esther! Why didn't I think of that before?'

Leif Panduro always looked worried in photos and in person. Now I saw him really smile for the first time. So that's what he looked like when he was happy. 'The solution was right under my nose the whole time. Esther tried to explain it to me but, idiot that I am, I didn't understand. Leif, that's me! Panduro is that writer fellow, the guy with the outdated view on women. My own view on women, Leif's view on women, is called Esther. And there's nothing old-fashioned about it! And if there is, Esther will take care of it herself.'

'What should I do about Puk?' I inquired.

'Give her a kiss for me. Puk Bonnesen, I'm not scared of you anymore. Watch out, Puk! Go tell your own stories, but be careful your view on men doesn't become outdated! When it does I'll come after you!'

THIRTEEN

Sometimes Life is Not a Fairy Tale

The person at the Factory who had the most powerful antidepressant effect on me is Puk. Puk was the only one of us who wrote essays.

It was no secret that I was extremely self-absorbed, in fact I advocated it as a kind of self-defence against depression. My self-centredness was so enormous that I was convinced that most of Puk's essays were about me.

On the surface they appeared to be cultural criticism, but I saw myself lurking beneath the surface. When she wrote about the modern, narcissistic personality I felt I was the target. Narcissism to her was tantamount to the erection of a false self, capable of dealing with kaleido-scopic modern life.

When she wrote about stupidity as a defence against chaos she used examples from my life.

To Puk boredom was a layer of grease, a shock absorber, that many people needed between themselves and the threatening real world. She always wrote about me, I thought.

It was always a comfort to meet people who felt the same way I did; they were sure she was writing about them. The reviewers usually claimed Puk was describing a generation.

People are always on their guard around Puk. Even Amanda, my depression, keeps a wary eye on her. Amanda is always on her best behaviour in Puk's presence and maintains a low profile.

What is it about Puk that's so intimidating? She's always perfectly civil, and it would never occur to her to scream or shout or use foul language.

Nobody ever comes right out and says they're afraid of Puk. How can you be afraid of a small, polite woman with large round eyes and a quiet voice?

Without Puk I would probably be dead today. I would have committed suicide. That statement is much too melodramatic for Puk's taste, but it's the truth.

Puk organizes. Puk arranges. Puk brings people together. Puk solves problems. Puk knows all the right people. People become the right people because they know Puk. She does it so easily and elegantly that it looks as though she's doing it for fun. She probably is, too.

Puk doesn't mind having fun, but it's not at the top of her wish list. Number one on her list is the desire to understand. She wants to understand everything.

Puk writes her novels and essays as though it was child's play. Every time she publishes a book there's a photo of her on the front page of *Politiken*. She was the youngest member to be elected to the Danish Academy.

I meet people everywhere who ask me what the *real* Puk Bonnesen is like. The answer is that she is precisely the person she seems to be. She has a good head, a sharp tongue and she's always courteous and friendly.

Puk gets an idea and before long she's carried it out. In my case she had the idea that it would be interesting to learn everything about my depression, about Amanda. She's never told me why and I've never asked. It makes my blood run cold to think that just one thought, one idea in the mind of a woman I didn't know, changed the course of my life. It's frightening and soothing at the same time. Or secure, as Puk would put it. Secure is her favourite word.

Puk created the Factory, our collaborative venture. She also decreed that we, the four proprietors, should never be friends in private. Friendships come to an end; the Factory must never end. Our mutual relationship had to last for the duration of our lives. When Puk speaks we don't just nod mechanically; we nod because we usually agree with her.

I can only guess what Puk thinks of me. What I think of her I keep to myself.

The reserve between us broke down one spring night thirteen years after we had founded the Factory. The living room phone in our apartment on Nansensgade rang and kept on ringing. I stumbled out of bed, half asleep, and answered it.

'Hello?'

'Dan?'

'Yes, who's speaking?'

'It's me,' whispered an almost inaudible voice.

'Who's me?'

'It's me. Can you come?'

I didn't recognize the voice. My immediate reaction was that it was a wrong number.

'Dan? Dan?'

'Yes, this is Dan.'

Then someone started crying on the other end.

'Hello?' I said. 'Who's calling? Are you sure you want to talk to Dan Moller?'

'Yes,' came the whisper.

'What do you want?'

'Help.'

Suddenly I was wide awake and fully alert. 'Puk?'

'Yes.'

'What happened?'

'Can you help me?'

'Of course I can help you.'

'It's so awful.'

'What's so awful?'

'Dan, come and help me.'

'Are you at home?'

'Yes.'

'I'm on my way.'

It took me less than a half-hour to get by taxi to Frederiksberg Allé where she lives with her husband and two young daughters.

Her apartment is near Sankt Thomas Square.

I rang the bell downstairs and she buzzed me in.

There was blood all over her face. One of her eyes was

swollen shut. She didn't say a word when I saw her. She knew I knew what had happened.

I wrapped her up in some clothes and carried her down to the street as though she was a rug.

We went back to Nansensgade by cab. Beate called Puk's brother Michael, whose practice is on Osterbrogade and lives close by. He came at once. He examined Puk. She had received multiple fist blows to the head. He advised her to go to the hospital. At 5 a.m. she was admitted to Rigshospitalet to be examined for a fractured skull.

Michael and I remained with her. Puk's children were at her husband's parents'.

Puk was heavily medicated and fell into a deep sleep.

Michael was the first to point out that he and I had been in a similar situation many years ago. It was long ago but we both remembered it clearly. It was when we had run into each other in the psychiatric ward at Rigshospitalet when we were both students living at Nordisk Kollegium on Strandboulevarden. I was a dental student back then and heavily medicated.

Groggy from the medication I had told him about my depression, how one night on an acid trip the depression had become a person, a woman, Amanda. That conversation completely changed the course of my life.

There are many encounters that do not take place by chance, but that meeting in the corridor of the psychiatric ward was as random as it gets. In spite of my drugged state I remembered every word we said. This was also because I later concluded that chance encounter was the turning point of my life.

Before we turned to the subject of Puk he wanted to hear how Amanda was doing. Amanda told Michael about the Salinger Syndrome. Michael was a neurologist. Depression is frequently considered a neurological disorder, an electrical-chemical signal imbalance of the neurones. He had no trouble understanding Amanda's account of the Salinger Syndrome: visual and auditory stimuli; difficulty processing all outside signals; imbalance of the how-to-please function. I didn't need the post office image to get Michael to understand.

Michael was now a physician-in-chief and I had become a writer. We had known each other a long time.

He wanted me to tell him the truth about Puk.

I snorted. 'The truth? How should I know the truth?'

Michael said: 'She's always kept a certain distance, you know that. Puk divides her world into compartments, separated by silent shutters. You know that.'

'Yes, I do know that.'

'Listen, Dan, it was no coincidence that you were the one she called.'

'No,' I sighed deeply.

'I know Puk would hate this, but I need to hear what you have to say, truth or not. She looks like someone almost killed her. A man she loves. Give it to me straight. Are you going to talk to me or not?'

'Michael, considering the fact that you once more or less saved my life I'll try to help you out.'

'Thanks, Dan, I would be very grateful.'

Before I told him anything I had to make a slightly embarrassing confession. It came as no surprise to Michael. 'You understand, Michael, I have no special views on your sister that could be of any interest. Apart from generalities I'm completely empty. Amanda's the one who knows everything. She has ideas. She's saved up countless experiences we've had with Puk including our own reactions. She can rewind the film and blow up every single detail in our life with Puk. Amanda never forgets a thing.'

'So you have to ask her?'

'Exactly.'

'Take your time. Both of you.'

'Puk is the person who's helped me most in my work with the Salinger Syndrome.'

'How so?'

'Because her *modus operandi* is so unequivocal. She divides all external signals into two categories: 'Useful' or 'Not useful'.

'Sounds like Puk,' muttered Michael. 'She saves every piece of information that might be relevant and catalogues it. Later on when she needs it in that little mafia organisation she's got going, she can pick and choose.'

'Exactly. She's the Marlon Brando of literature, the Vito Corleone of Danish letters.'

Michael nodded. 'So far so good. But that was no rival Mafia boss that smashed her face in.'

'No. She did it herself.'

'You mean she did that to herself?'

'No, not me. Amanda thinks so.'

'Tell Amanda she has to talk to me loud and clear. The world is complicated enough already.'

Michael wants Amanda to tell him about Puk.

'What can *I* tell you about Puk?' I asked. 'You're her brother. You know her much better than I do.'

Michael nodded. 'I know this is the third time she's been knocked around by a husband or a boyfriend. I just have no idea what goes on or how to keep it from happening again.'

'Why don't you call Nora? She's a woman and she knows Puk far better than I do.'

'Look, Dan. You and Amanda, you're the one Puk called.'

'What about Boris? Boris has known Puk much longer than I have, too.'

'That's it? You're telling me to call up all her friends, her admirers, the whole damn entourage? Puk and all the little Puks?'

'Yes, that was precisely what I was about to suggest.'

'Come on, Dan. It's up to you. You and Amanda.'

'Stop trying to dump this in my lap.'

'You and Amanda, buddy.'

There was no way out; Amanda and I had to pull ourselves together.

Puk was so well organised that she knew she'd need Amanda one day. Puk's talent was bringing people together and watching how they brought out the best in each other. This meant she needed to collect information and be willing to see things as they are. Amanda is more than competent at both these tasks.

Sitting with Puk's brother by her bedside at Rigshospitalet it was time to pay my debt.

All those years ago Puk had chosen Amanda and me. Puk had transformed my life; she may even have saved it.

A mafia boss had done me a favour. A debt was owed. The time had come to return that favour.

The favour consisted of doing what Puk did in her books. She deconstructed the world. She took the world apart, explained it and put all the parts together again. One of her most famous essays dealt with stupidity and boredom. Stupidity was not lack of intelligence. Boredom was the opposite of having fun. Stupidity and boredom were instruments people created as buffers between themselves and the world, a distance. She quoted Andy Warhol: 'My greatest wish is to become a machine.'

Now I had to deconstruct Puk. Take her apart, study all the parts and then put them together again. Two or three hundred things I know about Puk Bonnesen.

To be eligible for the deconstruction process a fact had to be relevant to the current situation. The current situation was that she had been the victim of severe abuse. Blows to the head and body. Furthermore it was not the first time. The unpleasant truth was that virtually all of Puk's lasting love relationships terminated in violence. The best brain in Danish literature had had more concussions caused by violence than her friends and family could bear to think about.

141

Michael listened patiently to our ideas, Amanda's and mine. What we actually thought of Puk.

We recalled all the times people had asked us: 'What's the *real* Puk Bonnesen like?'

The question was actually implied in the answer. There was no discrepancy between the Puk one met and the Puk behind the façade. There is no *real* Puk.

She's a successful author. She handles her talent and her career brilliantly. She's a master of organization and thinks it's fun to know everybody. She's the brain behind the Factory. As she says herself she has two children with four different husbands. She loves appearing on television on entertainment programs as well as cultural ones. She takes pleasure in being called the most powerful woman on the Danish intellectual scene. Her newspaper articles are studied thoroughly by everyone with power and influence. She's always obliging and friendly. She has friends everywhere. If she has any enemies they keep a low profile.

But now her brother and I were setting by her hospital bed as we had done several times before. The unofficial queen of the Danish intelligentsia had had her face bashed in.

Michael needed to know why. He had a hunch the only one who could provide an answer was Amanda, Amanda in collaboration with me.

Michael and I had played indoor soccer together for hours at Nordisk Kollegium. I knew how stubborn he was.

'I think you owe me a better answer than that,' he said finally.

'Why's that?'

'If it wasn't for me you wouldn't have had the brilliant literary career you enjoy today.'

'What kind of answer do you want?'

'You know.'

'No, honestly, I don't.'

'Remember you told me about the enzyme? That you spend your whole life in a little room in a laboratory studying the Salinger Syndrome?'

'You want me to explain to you why Puk always ends up getting beaten up by her lovers? Based on the Salinger Syndrome?'

'Well, I'm a neurologist. I could explain the world by means of neurology, couldn't I?'

Michael gave a knowing smile. He was a scientist and was fully aware this didn't require a great deal of effort on my part. I had it all wrapped and ready on a shelf in the lab. All I had to do was reach up to the top shelf and take it down. To be sure it was not a full-blown theory on Puk and physical violence, but it was a contribution to a theory.

The Salinger Syndrome model can be applied to anyone. All human beings constantly receive impressions from the outside world. How do they react? How do they process the impressions they receive? What signals do they transmit to the outside world in turn? Such signals are crucial in determining other people's reactions to the individual. People need to transmit certain signals in order to receive what every human being longs for: kindness, attention and love.

How does Puk Bonnesen go about getting what she needs from the surrounding world? What she wants is kindness, attention and love and what she gets is a face beaten to a pulp.

What does Salinger Syndrome theory have to say about that?

I knew the secret of Puk's talent, as a writer and as an organizer. Her receiving/transmitting mechanisms worked perfectly. She was able to receive and process external information to an extraordinary degree. Her information filter was in perfect working order. Anything that could be used was neatly catalogued and set aside for further use. All superfluous information was immediately bounced back into space. She was in no danger of being weighed down by useless knowledge. No one can use her as a dustbin for all the problems they want to get rid of. I've never met anyone so many people want to confide in. She's considered extraordinarily gifted. Countless times I've heard people say, 'And then I told Puk . . .' They think what they say remains within Puk, that she thinks about it, that it makes an impression on her, but I know what really happens. Puk examines what she hears for its nutritional value, its utility value. If she can't find any she gets rid of it as soon as possible before it becomes a dead weight. Other people are weighed down by information rotting inside them. Not Puk.

Puk's receptors are always up and running and she has no trouble transmitting, back to her surroundings, out of herself. Just like everyone else, she transmits a signal that will get her what she needs: friendship, attention and love.

What's special about Puk, from the perspective of the Salinger Syndrome, is her balance. All the individual components that make up the Salinger Syndrome are in perfect balance. All the information she's gathered and catalogued is transformed into outgoing energy. She uses the information to do people favours, to combine people, bring them together in combinations they would never have imagined on their own. It's Puk's way of showing kindness, of being attentive. Everyone who's on Puk's receiving end is happy, and is doubly friendly in return.

Michael was demonstratively quiet, staring at me fixedly. I knew what I had just said about Puk wouldn't satisfy him. If there was any way for me to sneak out of the hospital ward without saying another word it would be a relief, as he knew. I felt such strong affection for Puk lying in bed beside us and moving uneasily in her sleep that I couldn't make myself go on.

Michael took pity on me. 'Ok, is this what you're saying? That the Salinger Syndrome is brilliant when you apply it to your work? But the same system applied to your husband and children is a disaster?'

'Yes,' I whispered.

'When Andy Warhol wishes he were a machine he's talking about art, right? When you're in love with a machine it arouses emotions in people that drive them to violence in desperation.'

'Yes, that's pretty much it. If I wasn't ashamed of thinking such things about my good friend Puk.'

Michael raised his voiced. 'She's not your friend. Puk has no friends, just a large number of acquaintances. All her acquaintances know they're only acquaintances. But we, her family, we're desperate and unhappy because we're only pawns in Puk's great life work. And her life's work may end up getting her killed some day.'

'We all use each other, don't we?' I muttered.

'Spare me your psycho-babble!' Michael exploded. 'I need to know the truth if I'm to keep Puk from ending up dead some day.'

'Look, Michael. The Salinger Syndrome isn't the truth. It's my own hypothetical explanation of a narrowly defined type of depression. Puk isn't even depressed. It's just a theory and it may not apply to Puk at all. I could be wrong, although I don't think I am.'

Michael asked: 'Are you in love with Puk?'

That was easy. 'My feelings for her are very strong and clear. I admire her, I'm in love with her, and I love her. I am simply physically attached to her. Almost dependent on her.'

'Thank you, Dan, I needed to know that.'

'I needed to say it, too.'

FOURTEEN

What a Real Poet Looks Like

A portrait of Boris is a portrait of success. Boris Schauman is far and away the most successful author in Denmark. No one can touch him when it comes to media coverage, rave reviews, literary prizes, early membership of the Danish Academy, etc.

The author he's most often compared to is Ernest Hemingway. Boris had an aunt who was a friend of Karen Blixen, or Isaac Dinesen, as she called herself. As a child Boris frequently met Karen Blixen at the home of a clergyman in Helsingborg, a cousin of Bror Blixen, Karen Blixen's husband. Boris read and admired Hemingway. Karen Blixen had met Hemingway many times when she was living in Africa. She told Boris tales of Hemingway, as she put it. Hemingway did his best to come across as a Real Man, the embodiment of masculinity. When Blixen was in the presence of Hemingway she always pictured him in a dress. Everything Hemingway wrote had to do with being strong, brave, invulnerable. Beneath the façade he was an anxious woman who drank too much to dull his sensitivity. At the end he suffered from paranoia and depression. He was treated with electric shock therapy and committed suicide by blowing his brains out.

Wide-eyed, Boris sat in the rectory listening to Karen Blixen's stories about Hemingway.

He later found out that everything she had told him was true; it was no African fairy tale, as she might have said.

Boris can write in any genre and has. Is he best as a poet, a novelist or a dramatist? It's a moot question. However, there is universal agreement that he's the darling of the gods and has been since his literary debut at the age of 21. The gods gave him talent, looks, charm, good health, an even disposition. Physically he's built the way a romantic poet should be, tall, broad-shouldered, with a thick head of hair that he used to wear down to his shoulders when he was young. He was in the front ranks during the student uprising of 1968 and subsequently. He became a symbol of his generation. Compared to him poets who till then were said to represent the *Zeitgeist* suddenly became obsolete. To make sure no one was in any doubt he always wore floral trousers. He knew he too would become obsolete one day and looked forward to it. 'When I meet my successor I'll kill him.'

When the media wanted a statement from the world of Danish letters they would often turn to Boris. He could always be counted on to express an opinion that would create a stir.

When Boris walks down the street all heads turn in his direction. He's always friendly and affable so it can take a long time to reach the end of the street. People stand in line to greet him. They can't wait to comment on something he said or wrote. Some want his autograph or to have their picture taken with him. He's that rare phenomenon, the literary superstar. This he enjoys to the full.

Puk was right when she decided that the four of us at the Factory should keep our personal contact outside the office to an absolute minimum. Boris is successful and success breeds envy. Boris' personal friends pay a price. For some it's a small price to pay, but not for others. Being friends with Boris is like being a member of a clan or a clique. You're in danger of ceasing to be an autonomous individual; you're merely a friend of the famous writer.

Boris did all he could to defuse the situation. He was not arbitrary, he was not self-absorbed. Nevertheless he was the flame that attracts moths and moths get burnt.

This posed no threat to the rest of us. We were careful never to be seen with Boris outside the office. We never went out for a coffee or to a restaurant with him, we never attended the same social events. When we met we always greeted each other pleasantly but slightly formally.

Puk had got it right. Our joint collaboration had to last a lifetime. Envy is a lurking pitfall. If any of us were envious of Boris' success it had to be kept under strict control. The same rule applied if one of us was struggling with a problem the others could help with. No psychological ambulance service. No confidences. If we occasionally succumbed to the temptation to ask, 'How are you?' the answer was invariably, 'Oh, just great. Thanks.'

That was why it took me so long to find out what was underway in the spring of 1981.

It began when a number of my fellow writers started lining up for an appointment with me in the Botanical Gardens. The first was Dan Turell. We were the same age and had met here and there. We had our first name in common. He was the real Dan. When people heard I was a writer and my name was Dan, they always said, 'Oh, like Dan Turell.' The real Dan was a highly sensitive, shy man. He had resolved not to be anonymous; he was going to be a famous poet. So he decked himself out in a wide-brimmed hat, brightly coloured clothes and nail polish. When he walked down the street people noticed him. It didn't change the fact that he was an excellent poet and it didn't make him any less shy. I myself have never been in the least shy. What did Dan Turell want to talk to me about? We strolled around the Botanical Gardens for three quarters of an hour. He smoked 7 cigarettes and I never found out what he wanted.

The same thing happened a few days later. Another colleague of the same age, Hans Jorgen Nielsen, wanted an appointment in the Botanical Gardens. We had met many times before. I was a great admirer of his. I didn't tell him though. Like Dan Turell he was very shy. He was wearing a beautiful red jacket. We spoke a bit nervously about sports, pop music, haiku poetry and the Gastronomic Academy of which he was a member.

I never found out what he wanted either.

The third time was when Ebbe Klovedal Reich called to make an appointment in the Botanical Gardens. Another shy colleague hiding beneath a colourful façade. Another stroll in the garden, the conversation flitting between politics, architecture and mutual friends.

Not until we turned a corner and ran directly into Hans Jorgen Nielsen and Dan Turell did I realize anything was in the offing. I had no idea what direction it might take.

'This is an ambush,' said Dan Turell making a revolver out of his right hand.

The three colleagues looked at each other. They had agreed that Nielsen was their spokesman.

They had come because of a mutual friend, Boris.

'What about him?' I asked. 'Did he send you?'

The three musketeers shook their heads. Boris didn't know they had come. I had to promise not to tell him.

I promised.

Then they told me. They were here at the request of a woman they were all very fond of, Majken Suenson, Boris' wife.

'Why didn't she just call me herself?' I asked.

'You're the one that knows Boris best,' said Ebbe Reich.

'Me?'

Turell and Nielsen nodded. 'That's what Majken says.'

'So? What's up? Are they getting divorced?'

'No, worse than that,' said Dan Turell.

Then they took turns telling me what it was about.

Majken had been diagnosed with breast cancer. She would tell Boris herself, of course, but there was something else she also had to tell him. While Boris had had a large number of mistresses over the years he could always count on Majken being at home. She was his anchor, his safe haven, mother of their three children. Boris loved Majken, no one was ever in any doubt of that. Now three of the husbands of Boris' many women had taken an initiative. They wanted Boris to know that for all those years his wife, Majken, had had what they called a 'friend.' Boris had to be told that his wife had cancer and he also needed to hear that his wife had had a secret lover for all those years.

'How do I come into the picture?' I said. Even though I knew perfectly well how I came into the picture.

The picture was that Majken wanted to protect Boris. So she asked her good friends Turell, Nielsen and Reich for help.

I had stopped smoking many years before. The three colleagues were chain-smokers. They offered me a fag and we stood there on the path in the Botanical Gardens, puffing away.

My three fellow authors all talk very fast and I myself speed up in many situations. We were all talking at once, but we could hear what the others were saying.

We were sorry Majken was ill, but the idea of Boris and his loving wife, who even now wanted to protect the poet genius, made our collective blood boil.

To reveal what my colleagues said would be a breach

of privacy as well as professional confidentiality. I can, however, relate what I said myself:

'You devious sons of bitches! In a few minutes you'll just walk out of the Botanical Gardens with a clear conscience. You've dumped the whole thing in my lap. You really are a bunch of assholes! I feel like shit!'

They completely agreed. They smiled, embraced me and hurried out of the Gardens.

Majken was right. I was the right man for the job. Majken is a realistic woman. She has a shop where she sells imported kitchen equipment with her sister and cousin. Being the wife of a lionised author is not easy. Being the wife of a man who's always falling in love with other women doesn't make it any easier. What Majken knew or didn't know, or chose not to know, is something nobody knows, at least I don't. The only reason I regret not being a personal friend of Boris is that I never see Majken.

Majken had now sent me a message through complicated channels. She knew of course I wouldn't refuse. For one thing, as she well knew, I was such a big fan of Nielsen, Turell and Reich that I would pay good money just to be in their presence. Any one of them could persuade me to do anything. And all three of them! I didn't stand a chance!

I am a fairly cold person, at best my character is temperate. The situation did not cause me any great agitation or leave me in any doubt. I knew immediately what I had to do.

Many depressed people keep depression at bay by confronting the realities of a situation head on.

I returned to the Factory and did something I'd never done before. I knocked on the door to Boris' office and went in. He was bent over his desk, his back to me.

'We need to talk,' I said.

He turned around. I could tell he knew I didn't bring good news.

I told him then what I had come to tell him, what our three fellow authors had told me.

He looked at me and blinked. He kept looking at me and blinking.

Then he got up and put on his coat which was hanging on a hook on the wall. Before he left he waved the index finger of his right hand at me a couple of times in parting. We know each other so well he didn't have to tell me what he was thinking.

For the next three weeks Boris and I met every evening in the neighborhood where Frederiksborgvej intersects Rentemestervej, in the northwest section of Copenhagen.

Boris and Majken had lived in a commune there during their first years together. We wandered the streets and always ended our session by having coffee in a café.

When people know each other as well as Boris and I do the most important thing is not what's said but what's not said. He knows what I think and I know what he thinks. We skipped the preliminaries and went straight for the jugular, the solution.

He said what he always says when he has a problem: 'What does Amanda think?'

I knew what Amanda thought but, considering the state Boris was in, I had to discuss the whole thing with her thoroughly before presenting it.

Boris did the hard work himself. He knew what I would refuse to listen to: I didn't want to hear the story of his life. I didn't want to hear one word about the turmoil raging inside him. I didn't want to hear how ridiculous he felt, like a spoiled child, a pompous writing fool. I offered him not one drop of understanding, empathy or forgiveness. I was my usual dry, unpleasant self, myself in fact.

He didn't write a word during that time. He also became sexually impotent.

I refused to listen to that too. There were only two things I wanted to hear: What did he think of Amanda's theories? How was he going to apply my theories on the Salinger Syndrome?

Both Amanda and Salinger caused him pain, I could see. He suffered and I let him suffer. Especially because Amanda and Salinger said pretty much the same thing.

They both raised the subject of Boris's genitals, his cock and balls. Boris has written so much about his genitals that they're a recurring element in the Danish Teachers Association's notes to Boris' work. Boris writes about sex. Sex is the source of his creative energy. One of his early mistresses called his genitals Fido and the Twins. Several times in the 1970s Boris appeared in films produced by his friends. Nude scenes were fine with him. That way everyone could admire Fido and the Twins, Laurel and Hardy.

Boris could only write when he was in love, sexually involved in his newest conquest. Everyone knew that.

Now Fido and the Twins had taken a hit. There was no need to bring Puk and Nora into it. They were red-blooded, red-stocking feminists. We knew what they thought. They were fond of Boris, but when it came to sexual politics they thought he was a jerk.

Amanda and the Salinger Syndrome had to find a way forward and out, instead of downwards into the hell of self-contempt towards which he was heading at high speed.

Amanda said Boris should unscrew Fido, put him in the freezer and wait for better times.

This was unmitigated cruelty, I felt.

Amanda pointed out that Boris used sex as a drug and should go cold turkey immediately.

But what if that meant Boris never wrote another word?

Amanda said: 'Does he have to spread his seed over the whole town for his name to go down in literary history?'

Boris didn't answer.

Amanda continued: 'He who has sex with a thousand women has sex with no one.'

Boris mumbled something Amanda didn't hear.

Boris did most of the thinking himself, Amanda restricted herself to raking him over the coals.

I brought up the only subject that really interests me, the Salinger Syndrome. Boris could see it coming. We both knew that was why we were spending hour after hour together around Rentemestervej.

Boris is a true artist. Whatever he experiences, whatever he sees or hears is translated into art. His system is never overloaded by too many impressions. He can't experience enough.

My area of specialisation within Salinger Syndrome Theory is the how-to-please mechanism. It had worked perfectly for Boris until now. His soul was never in any doubt how to go about getting the attention and admiration he craved. He wrote, he charmed, he kissed, he hugged. His how-to-please mechanism got him more friendship, attention and love than anyone else in his generation perhaps.

Now it had all broken down. He held himself in the greatest contempt. When he read what he had written all he could see was an air of self-congratulation. When people greeted him on the street he felt he was being assaulted.

When he thought of Majken he saw himself as an overgrown baby, strutting about, his hand firmly grasping Fido.

Amanda and I quickly tired of watching Boris flagellating himself.

His self-flagellation took the form of claiming that self-flagellation was just as infantile as any other kind of sexual perversion.

That was when Boris touched bottom in his despair and slowly began to surface.

He did it with the help of the only thing I had to offer: a means of regulating the Salinger Syndrome's how-to-please mechanism.

Boris sighed when he heard it. 'That's the most unsexy thing I ever heard in my life. You won't mind if I start crying, will you?'

But it was the lever he needed to keep from drowning in self-pity and despair.

No more admiration. No more acclaim. No more literary prizes. No charming TV appearances. No in-depth interviews for the papers.

Then came the worst part, the part that hurt most, the part Amanda delighted in telling him. 'No beautiful young women to seduce and conquer. No falling in love, no infatuations.'

Boris looked as though he was about to cry when he said: 'No more sex?'

Amanda said. 'Boris you're not seven years old anymore. You have a wife you love. She needs your help. Try to think about her a little more and a little less about Fido and the Twins.'

Boris was crying in earnest now. He whispered: 'You could have spared me that last remark, you bitch. *Fuck you, Amanda. Fuck you to hell*!'

FIFTEEN

Portrait of a Lightweight

One day Puk received a request. This was nothing new, Puk is always receiving requests. She never told us how the requests reached her, perhaps at a dinner party, or a friend of a friend may have called her.

Puk received a request from a woman writer who was encountering major difficulties in the novel she was writing. She needed help. It was a well known fact throughout the literary world that Puk was the one to see if you were having trouble with a novel. Puk would find the best man for the job.

Puk handed me a manuscript and asked me to read it. She'd only tell me who had written it if I accepted.

The novel was about the breakdown of a marriage. I had only read two sentences and I knew who the author was. The novel's stumbling blocks were purely structural and easily fixed. I drafted my alterations and met with Tove Ditlevsen in the Botanical Gardens. She was 54 when I met her in 1971. She was a well known and much loved writer and editor. Before we met I had to promise two things: never to tell anyone what she and I discussed, neither in writing nor verbally, and never to mention it in a private diary.

She explained why she felt so strongly about it. The letters she had written to friends and lovers over the years had been bought up by a collector. When she called the collector and reproached him she was told he had done it for financial reasons. He believed her current popularity would hold and one day she would be just as famous as Soren Kierkegaard and Hans Christian Andersen. He asked her if she realized what Andersen's and Kierkegaard's letters were going for these days.

I promised everything she told me would be in strictest confidence. That was easy enough because she told me nothing about her private life. I enjoyed that day in the Botanical Gardens. We discussed her manuscript; she approved my revisions.

Not until we were bidding each other goodbye did she mention Nora From, my dear colleague at the Factory, as she called her. She knew Nora very, very well, she said. But she always found it a little irritating when Nora was called the new Tove Ditlevsen.

'For Christ's sake! I'm not dead yet, am I?'

I replied that not only was she very much alive, she was also a very beautiful woman.

Then she told me something that made my blood run cold, and walked off.

Nora writes drama, film and theatre. She's an expert at cliffhangers. The heroine is holding onto the edge of the cliff with her fingernails. While she's hanging there the scene cuts to somewhere else. The spectators remain glued to their seats. They have to find out what happens to the heroine. Will she be saved or will she plunge to her death on the rocks below?

Tove Ditlevsen's parting remark was just such a cliffhanger.

Cut to Nora.

The Factory rules stipulated we must never comment on each other's work. Another absolute taboo was any mention of reviews, either our own or the others'.

For the fun of it we always concealed a wink at the others in all our work. For my part I always worked in the three others as secondary characters, disguised of course and under different names.

I wouldn't dream of telling them, but I was sure I was the others' favorite model. I was the character with obsessive-compulsive disorder, the one who catalogues whatever he experiences, the one without the slightest sense of humor, or the phantom seeking a pair of eyes and a voice - the character that's just a little out of sync.

All of Nora's comedies were based on living models. She would often disguise me as a woman or a rabbit or a teddy bear. They were all slightly inept and were always on the lookout for friendship and love. She wrote romantic comedies. When the main characters are united in the end, the ugly duckling has long since become a swan.

Nora never mentioned the word depression. She never gave me explicit advice. She leaves little gifts lying around that I can open or not as I choose. When I watch her working with actors she tells them things I know are directed at me.

161

She's developed her own technique for analysing the relationship between two people. This is a tool actors use. It's called: 'How do I stay centre stage?'

The other side of that question is: 'How do I keep everyone else offstage?'

Nora has collected so much material over the years that she could write an instruction manual on how to be the centre of attention.

The whole thing boils down to this: when to listen, when not to listen.

Another theory she had was the drinking straw theory. Some people are like drinking straws, she told the actors. They dip their straw into other people and suck them dry. She said, 'You meet a friend, a so-called friend. When you're finished talking to this friend you're so exhausted you can hardly crawl. What happened? Your good friend drained you of your last drop of energy. How was it done and what does it teach us?'

Nora is an expert on social interaction. When she meets people who want to be more intimate with her than she does with them, she smiles a special smile: very cordial, very warm. Behind the smile she's readying the scalpel to surgically sever the relationship at precisely the right moment.

Nora's acting directions always have a profoundly anti-depressant effect on me.

Nora is a lightweight, she says so herself. Her only agenda is to entertain. She says she wants to be the Marilyn Monroe of literature. Who wants to see Marilyn

Monroe in a tragedy? We want to see her in comedies. Nora wouldn't dream of being profound. She loves superficial entertainment herself. She writes for success and money.

Our personalities are diametrically opposed. I couldn't be funny if someone was pointing a gun to my head. When I talk, people never laugh, they frown. No one has ever called me charming. When people are trying to be nice they say, 'Nice talking to you, it's been, uh, very informative.'

Nora has no trouble finding material for her comedies. She begins with what's right under her nose. She started out as a journalist. She got married and had two sons. Her husband cheated on her and they were divorced. That divorce proved a gold mine for Nora. She's written two novels about it, three collections of short stories and two plays. She's even written a musical about the divorce. All highly successful. She would often say: 'The marriage was a disaster, but the aftermath was a success.'

Her sons, Max and Jacob, are the most important things in her life, but so are the good reviews and all the money she's made since the break-up of her first marriage.

Later she married a businessman, Nicklas, who's in the carpet business. The marriage is apparently a success; Nora hasn't written a word about it.

Nora has directed her plays and films herself for many years. As soon as she gets an idea she acts on it. When she thought it might be fun to be a director she went straight to Sam Besekow and knocked on his door. She did the same thing later with the director Palle Kjærulff-Schmidt.

Nora loves social gatherings. She loves to cook. Even though she's thin as a rake she loves to prepare food, eat food and discuss food.

She takes great care drawing up her guest lists.

This is only hearsay of course since I've never been invited to any of her dinner parties, nor have the two others. Rules are made to be observed. Particularly Puk Bonnesen's rules.

What Puk doesn't know and what Boris only suspects is that Nora and I are secretly friends. We're personal friends even though it's strictly forbidden.

When we really get going we tell each other we're each other's best friend.

In Nora's case I know it isn't true. It's just something she says to make me happy.

It's a clandestine friendship. There's no love interest, no sex. There's only the pleasure of being together. We have secret places where we meet.

I tell Nora everything. I used to think she told me everything.

Nora teaches me all kinds of antidepressant things. She's taught me more antidepressant techniques than anyone else. Before Nora took me in hand I was incapable of making small talk, chattering with people I didn't know. I was so unresponsive that people would willingly have killed me. She taught me how to have a casual conversation. She directed me the way a director directs an actor. I didn't have a spark of talent but with Nora's help I could just about manage to talk about the weather and ask how things are going.

Nora taught me the most antidepressant technique I've ever learnt. She uses it when writing and directing comedies and also in her personal life. Just like everything else, she says, she stole it from somebody else, in this case from the French philosopher, Henri Bergson. Bergson claims that all comedy derives from the breakdown of rigid, mechanical behaviour. All human beings, all events proceed according to a built-in mechanical system. Instinctively we know what to expect from a normal procedure, and then when the expected mechanism breaks down, we're surprised, we're liberated, and we laugh.

I stole it from Nora as soon as I heard it, who had stolen it from Bergson, who had probably stolen it from someone else. Ideas are made to be stolen and I quickly made it mine. I apply it a hundred times a day and it works every time. Unfortunately my wife and daughters find it extremely irritating since it has certain consequences: I'm incapable of following an instruction manual, I never follow recipes, and worst of all I always cross on red.

Blaming it on Woody Allen is just a bad excuse. Nora had heard about Bergson from Woody Allen.

Woody was in Copenhagen one spring, staying with Mia Farrow and four of her adopted children at the Hotel d'Angleterre. He had checked in under an alias and wanted to be left in peace. The family was on their way home from Stockholm where he had met Ingmar Bergman, his idol.

Nora was a great admirer of Woody Allen and had been ever since she'd seen his first movie, *Bananas*. Woody Allen was her role model as a writer and a director.

Woody Allen is a genius, Nora maintained, even though some of his work was not the work of a genius, of course, just like all geniuses.

Nora's favorite Woody Allen quotation was, 'Whenever I start on a new project I look around and ask myself what does it remind me of that was highly successful?'

Woody's sole reason for coming to Denmark was Soren Kierkegaard. Woody had read Kierkegaard ever since he was very young. He identified with Kierkegaard. Kierkegaard had been his gateway to two other existentialists, Sartre and Heidegger. Woody was the world's most famous professional neurotic. He claimed he dealt in neuroses; neuroses had made him a rich man. He claimed to suffer from anhedonia himself, a lack of the ability to enjoy. He found the same anhedonia in Kierkegaard, which is why he was in Denmark for a few days to see everything he could relating to Kierkegaard. Puk saw to it that Woody's guide to Kierkegaard was Nora.

Nora took him to the Copenhagen City Museum on Vesterbrogade where the few things Kierkegaard left behind are on exhibit. This doesn't amount to more than a few pieces of furniture. Woody had looked at the furniture and whispered to Nora, 'I'm so moved I could cry, but I never cry on principle.'

Nora later wrote a newspaper article about her meeting with Woody Allen in which he maintained he was ashamed of being a comedian. 'It's like when you're invited to a party and they put you at the children's table.' He hoped he would grow up one day and write bleak dramas but he knew it would never happen. The title of the article was 'Study in Silence.' Woody never laughed, he was very quiet. 'Laughter is work,' he explained, 'Funny is money.'

Woody explained Bergson's theories while they were looking at Kierkegaard's furniture at the Copenhagen City Museum.

I've never told anyone about my eyes and voice issues except Nora. She had a theory that working with the automatic and the mechanical might help.

I don't experience anything until I've told my wife. I see the world through my wife's eyes. I've borrowed her eyes. When you don't have eyes of your own you don't have a voice either. I borrow other people's voices. There are four voices I borrow from in turn, my three Factory colleagues and my wife.

Nora is working on it. She believes that my own eyes will have a breakthrough one day. On that day my depression will disappear, says Nora. She knows perfectly well that's not what happens in real life, only in one of Nora From's charming comedies.

Being in a comedy by Nora From is one of the best things that ever happened to me. Written by Nora, directed by Nora. A shallow, hopelessly romantic comedy in which the lovers are united in the end, and the bad guys have to leave town.

I don't have to actually be with Nora for her to have a tonic effect on me. Simply knowing she's there is an upper. If I need to, I can see her and tell her what's bothering me. That's a pick-me-up in itself.

Who loves Nora? Everybody loves Nora. When I hear people talk about her they always go on about how wonderful she is, how great it must to be friends with her. I feel that way myself.

Cut back to Tove Ditlevsen walking away from me down the street that day. What Tove had told me knocked me on the head like a boomerang. The boomerang was the phrase 'Everybody loves Nora.'

Three apparently innocent words, but they hit me full force. After talking to Tove the phrase 'Everybody loves Nora' sounded like a terminal illness, a death sentence.

It was cruel. She had made me see Nora with fresh eyes, Tove's eyes.

Why did Tove tell me and no one else? I'd known the answer to that one for years. People with depression are so hard-hit to begin with that one more depressing fact won't make any difference.

I kept what Tove had told me bottled up inside for a while before I could find a way of bringing it up with

Nora. There was no way I could call her up and say, 'Hey Nora, there's something we need to discuss.'

Eleven days passed before the right opportunity arose. During the course of those eleven days I thought about Nora constantly, so often that actually confronting her almost began to feel unnecessary. I knew so much about her now that all I had to do was reshuffle the pieces with Nora's name and put them together again to form a new picture.

Poor Nora. She had no suspicion I was springing a trap from which she couldn't escape. I was going to make her do something she would hate more than anything else in the world: take a long, hard look at herself.

For many years we had met in Tivoli on August 4th. We took turns choosing the restaurant where we'd have lunch and the rides we'd go on before lunch. This time I chose a ride on the boats in the lake near the Chinese Pagoda.

In mid-lake I had Nora where I wanted her. If she tried to get away, she'd have to jump into the lake.

'Tove Ditlevsen tells me you're a junkie.'

Nora was rowing. The smile on her lips didn't falter an inch. She didn't even glance in my direction.

The important thing was that now Nora knew I knew she was an addict. She also knew I knew *why* she was an addict.

She knew I had spent a large portion of my life studying one small mechanism: the how-to-please mechanism. She knew I had studied it so intensely because my own mechanism is out of balance, causing my depression. She also knows that I know just about everything worth knowing about her own how-to-please strategies.

'So?' she asked.

'How long have you been a junkie?'

'Let's call it a consumer of cocaine, shall we?'

'My guess is seven years', I said.

'Four years, maybe five.'

'Does your husband know?'

'No. '

'Who knows?'

'Tove Ditlevsen, my pusher, and now you.'

'What should I do with this information?' I asked.

'I want you to be my accomplice, my witness. Dan, you must realize how relieved I am that now you know, too.'

'Did you send Tove Ditlevsen to tell me?'

'Of course not.'

'All that about my helping her with her manuscript, did that come from you?'

'Danny, sweetheart, that's how we make a living. Fiction, right?'

'Nora, if it wasn't Hans Christian Andersen's birthday I would strangle you and throw you in the lake.'

She laughed. 'It's not because of Andersen! The real reason is you've just been given the greatest proof of trust and affection a friend can give.'

'It weighs on me so heavily I'm afraid I'll sink straight to the bottom.'

'Great, you'll meet the little mermaid down there, Dan, and you can fall in love with her.'

That was the extent of our exchange on the subject of her drug abuse. Nora is not one for psychology in her personal life. She spouts psychology in everything she writes or directs, but when it comes to herself she's silent as the grave. Nobody better dare psychoanalyse *her*! If anyone tries, that's the last they see of her. She leaves the introvert stuff to me, she says. Other people's problems are like weeds, she maintains. People should keep their weeds in their own backyards.

That's why she sent Tove. Or Tove had sent herself. When I went over in my mind what I knew about Tove, it became clear to me she was the obvious choice.

It was a well known fact around town that Tove Ditlevsen was a drug addict and suffered from depression. Much of what she wrote dealt with ways in which she blackmailed her husbands and lovers into giving her the love she craved. She threatened them. She pleaded with them for love and attention. When that failed she twisted their arms to give her what she needed even more than drugs.

Nora gets more attention, friendship and love than anyone else I know. This applies to her work and to her private life. She knows how to gain people's confidence and win their devotion. I tease her by saying she's a small, highly efficient how-to-please machine. She finds this amusing, but refuses to listen to a single detail of my endless theories about her.

171

Nora's many friends miss her when they're not with her. They count the days before they can see her again. They feel like calling her every day but they know she's busy and that she has other friends. Everyone knows pretty much where they stand on Nora's friends list.

If they're in any doubt they can check out her dinner party guest list. Everyone in her milieu knows exactly who's invited. They keep count of who's been invited many times, just a few times or almost never. I know, too. It's easy for me to say because I'm never invited myself. Neither is Boris or Puk, of course, which is a comfort.

I also know how habitués react when for some unaccountable reason the invitations stop coming. Several have become so desperate they've approached me to find out what's going on. Did we say something wrong? Has Nora started to find us boring? Does Nora disapprove of our other friends? Whenever anyone approaches me I give the same answer: Nora never tells me her opinion of other people. That's a downright lie, of course. We hardly ever talk of anything else at our clandestine meetings. We exchange gossip by the truckload, and solemnly swear never to say anything nice about anybody.

We make a living off fiction, says Nora, fiction and vanity. We're both great believers in vanity. That's one of the many reasons we like Hans Christian Andersen so much. Unlike us he never tried to conceal his vanity. Andersen would go for a walk and catch sight of an acquaintance on the other side of the street. He'd cross the street and say, 'Hello. Now they're reading me in Spain now, too. Goodbye.' This was the Andersen Nora and I respected, and one of the reasons we commemorated the date of his death in Tivoli every year.

What did Andersen want? The same thing the rest of us want: attention, friendship and love. He was just less devious about it than the rest of us.

I can give Nora the same kind of attention I give Boris and Puk: Amanda. Without Amanda I would never have got near them.

In Nora's company Amanda became virtually invisible. Nora is number one on my list of anti-depressant friends.

She's at the top of my list and many other people's for the same reason she became a junkie. Amanda and I both know why, but usually we don't give it much thought.

We're facing it now though, surrounded by the rides, restaurants and entertainments of Tivoli Gardens the sole purpose of which is to please. The urge to please is a necessity of life, but once you've tried it you're hooked.

Nora, look the other way. I'm going to analyse you according to the Salinger Syndrome. I know you hate it. But you've chosen me for a friend because you know I can do it. That's why you sent Tove Ditlevsen to me.

And that's why you know I can handle your dirty little secret, because I know things, I've been there. And that's why you have to accept that you've become a case in my lifelong little research project, the Salinger Syndrome.

I too know what it's like, the urge to please. I just

173

never manage to please anybody. Of the four of us at the Factory I'm the worst. I wish things were different, but they're not.

You were a junkie long before you started snorting cocaine, Nora. You were hooked on popularity, on other people's admiration, on their love for you. You were a love abuser for so many years that you kept craving a higher dose. But then even that wasn't enough and you turned to synthetic love, drugs.

Nora, I don't know what to do. You probably have your habit under control just like everything else in your life. Except your love abuse, that is.

Hans Christian Andersen died on August 4th, 1875. Marilyn Monroe died on August 5th, 1972. Tove Ditlevsen died in 1971. Nora From is still alive.

SIXTEEN

Broome Street, New York

The telephone rang in our hotel room on Broome Street at 11.30 p.m.

Beate was lying on the bed, reading. She picked up the receiver. 'Yes?' Someone on the other end said something I couldn't catch and I couldn't read the expression on Beate's face. 'Yes,' she said evenly, 'Yes. I understand.'

She put her hand over the receiver and looked over at me. I was sitting in the window sill looking down at the street.

'It's them,' she said.

'Who?'

'Art Goldman and Rose.'

'What do they want?'

'To meet up with us.'

'When?'

'Now.'

'Where?'

'Down in the lobby.'

'Where are the letters?'

'Take it easy.'

Beate pulled up her sweater to reveal a money belt. It looked as if she was carrying a concealed weapon.

Instead of a weapon she had a bundle of letters strapped to her waist.

'How angry at them are we?' she asked.

'I'm furious at them.'

'They won't cheat us again.'

'How can you be so sure?'

'It's just a feeling I have.'

'Are those the genuine letters?'

'Sure are.'

'Can Art be sure of that?'

'No. And that's why they're going to play nice this time.'

'So you've got the whole thing figured out?'

'Dan, we've lived together for almost a lifetime. You know what I'm like. I'm that boring little dentist who always makes sure you don't trip over your own two feet more than absolutely necessary. I'm also the dentist of choice to all the big time crooks at home, maybe because I have a natural talent for crime.'

'You make me feel like an idiot.'

'You're not. It's just that you spend most of your life in your own thoughts.'

'What do we do now?'

'It depends on what you want,' replied Beate.

'I want revenge!'

'No you don't. I know what you want.'

'And what might that be?'

'You want to meet Salinger. The real Salinger.'

'Yes. That's true.'

'Well, you will,' she said.

'How can you be so sure?'

'I've read his letters too. Several times, actually.'

'When?'

'While you were asleep. I think I have a pretty good idea what Salinger's like. His letters are almost better than his books. When he writes about Kierkegaard he's fantastic.'

Beate got up from the bed and we left the room.

Down in the lobby Art and Rose were waiting for us. They beamed at us as if we were old friends finally getting together after a long absence, as they hurried to explain how they had only been obeying orders and assured us of their fondness for us. We were such a lovely family from wonderful Copenhagen.

Once the preliminaries were out of the way we sat down at a small table by the window facing Broome Street.

Rose Goldman and Beate did most of the talking.

Beate had brought her little yellow notebook and a ballpoint. She wrote down four conditions, pointing with the ball point to each condition as it was being negotiated. When agreement had been reached she moved the ballpoint to the next condition and resumed negotiations.

The whole thing didn't take very long. When Beate reached across the table to shake Rose's hand we all immediately stood up and said good bye.

A car was waiting for them on Broome Street.

Beate and I went up to our room. She brushed her teeth, put on her nightgown and quickly fell asleep. I lay awake all night.

Art Goldman's instructions were very simple. The next morning he called at the appointed time and said, 'Be at Battery Park tomorrow morning at 10. Take the ferry over to Ellis Island and the Statue of Liberty. You'll meet Jerry Salinger there. Remember to bring the letters.'

There wasn't a cloud in the sky when I arrived in Battery Park at the stroke of 10. There were a great many tourists, American and foreign.

I tried not to swivel my head from side to side in an attempt to catch a glimpse of Salinger. I kept my head turned front and restricted myself to peeking out of the corner of my eye. There were at least 20 men I thought were Salinger.

I took the ferry to Ellis Island and went with the tourist flow. I had been there several times before. No one came near me. No one spoke to me. I took the ferry over to the Statue of Liberty and climbed to the top.

No Salinger. I took the ferry back to Manhattan and then back again to Ellis Island. On Ellis Island I walked over to a bench near the water. From there I could see the Manhattan skyline bathed in bright morning light.

A man sat down next to me on the bench. I jumped about an inch, but it was only a German from Hamburg asking if I knew the best way to get to New Jersey. The funny thing was that the man looked like Salinger.

We chatted about Danish soccer players. Then his

wife came over with some friends and they left shortly afterwards.

I returned to the Statue of Liberty, and went back up into the head. It was very crowded but suddenly a space became available by the railing when an Indian woman in a yellow sari turned around and walked toward the exit. I hurried over to take her place.

A man was standing next to me. The first thing I noticed about him was the smell of the after shave or soap he used. It was a pleasant smell and reminded me of my father. The next thing I noticed was the man's hands. They were resting on the railing in front of him. The right hand turned toward me and made a small, discreet waving gesture.

I turned around and looked into the face of J.D. Salinger.

What had I expected? I was prepared to meet an angry, vengeful man. I had a clear picture of him based on the descriptions I had read in various newspapers and magazines over the past couple of years. He was described as a white-haired old madman obsessed with protecting his privacy from a curious public. The books written about him did not portray him in a favourable light. A young mistress had written a book about their love affair. His daughter had written a book about her difficult, paranoid father. A woman from Texas who met with him for a short time on a bridge near his home described him as clearly suffering from paranoia.

And here was I, who had travelled a long way to

blackmail him in the worst possible way. All the kindness and trust he had shown me in the letters we had written each other I was now using to blackmail him. It was not a pretty story, but I was just one of an endless number of paparazzi lying in wait to spring on him.

I would have understood if he had held me in the deepest contempt. I was prepared for it. But how do you prepare yourself? You set your expectations at an absolute minimum. You figure, 'OK, even if the man hates and despises me, and rightly so, it's worth it. I've dreamed of meeting him for so many years. No matter how unpleasant or disappointing this turns out to be, I want it to happen. I haven't travelled so far to go home empty-handed.'

I pictured a white-faced, thin-lipped old man, hatred burning in his eyes, his mouth distorted with anger, snarling his contempt for me. I imagined the spittle spraying from his lips as he raged at me. He would ask me for the letters and I would get what I'd come for, an interview. A violation of his privacy. The privacy he had tried to protect all his life. But I would have got what I came for. I would see Salinger *live*, just once in my life. And I would ask myself why I was doing it. And as always whenever I asked myself that question, I wouldn't know the answer.

I simply didn't know why I was doing it. I only knew it was something I craved, and now, up in the head of the Statue of Liberty, with a full view of Manhattan, it was finally happening.

And it was completely different from what I had imagined.

What happened was that I fell in love with the man at my first sight of him. Falling in love is the correct term, the only means of describing what I felt. It means that I became infatuated with him, I was crazy about him, I felt the deepest devotion towards him.

It occurred immediately. I felt a hand on my shoulder. I turned and looked into the face I knew so well. I had seen all the photographs of him available to the public, from photographs of him as a young man to the photographs two French photographers had taken recently in a parking lot after Salinger had been shopping. Salinger was angry and started threatening them. They had photographed the furious man from inside the car. It looked like a wanted poster more than anything else.

Salinger was an elderly man. His hair was still black streaked with white. His face was unchanged. The surprising thing was that he appeared to be enjoying himself, he seemed in excellent spirits, and he was friendly. He looked at me as though he had really looked forward to meeting me. The sun was shining and we were meeting at last! From the very first moment it was as though we were confidential old friends who had happily anticipated finally meeting.

He was my height, a little over 6 foot. He was wearing a light-coloured windbreaker. Underneath he was wearing a blue sweater and a light blue shirt. His pants were dark blue and he was wearing red sports shoes.

Red sports shoes! J.D: Salinger in a pair of smart, red sports shoes! Wow!

What had I expected? He would turn up in a coat of mail? In a uniform? Wearing a cassock?

He looked like a thousand other ordinary old men on a trip to Ellis Island and the Statue of Liberty.

Nobody gave him a second look. Nobody knew who he was. He looked completely ordinary.

Was it only because I was so fascinated by him that I thought he was anything but ordinary?

To me he was something special. In the first place he was handsome. He was simply a handsome old man. His eyes were dark and lively. He had charisma, he had an aura. Wherever that comes from. Mostly from his eyes, I think. His eyes were interested, attentive, but the rest of him was also so intensely present that you couldn't help feeling the energy emanating from him.

He stood next to me and looked out over Manhattan. I didn't want to be rude and just stand there gaping at him so I turned and looked out at New York too. New York was wonderful that morning but what I really wanted was to drink in the man standing next to me.

How much time would Salinger give me? Would he suddenly disappear? There was no way I could ask. Maybe he would disappear the minute I gave him the letters.

I felt I couldn't ask him for an interview either. It might scare him off.

And what did I want to ask him? What time did he

get up in the morning? What did he have for breakfast? Did he still smoke? What did he do for fun? Did he work out to keep in shape? What time did he go to bed? How many hours a night did he sleep? Was he in good health?

A bunch of ridiculous questions, but I was dying to ask.

He said, 'I brought the letters.'

I thought I'd heard wrong. I thought he asked me if I had brought the letters.

So I answered, 'Yes, I've brought the letters.'

He smiled, 'Dan, I don't think you understand.'

'Understand what?'

'*I've* brought the letters for *you*.'

'You mean the copies my wife had made of your letters?'

He shook his head. 'No, the genuine ones.'

'But I've got the genuine ones.'

He smiled even more widely. 'No, I've got the genuine ones, Dan.'

'I'm sorry, I don't understand what you mean.'

'Looks that way.'

I said, 'The letters I gave you, or rather your double, were only copies.'

He nodded. 'I'm aware of that.'

'What letters are you talking about then?'

He laughed. 'You have a very intelligent wife, Dan. I know all about that.'

'How do you know all about that?'

Salinger leaned forward and pointed toward

183

mid-Manhattan. 'Try looking down there, north of the Empire State Building, that green area down there. Can you see where I'm pointing? I was born there and lived there as a kid, Riverside Drive.'

'Yes, I've been inside your old building too.'

'Have you?'

'Yes.'

'I go there myself occasionally when I'm in New York.'

'You either visit William Shawn at the New Yorker or your sister Doris.'

Salinger laughed. 'Do you know where I stay when I'm in New York too?'

'Yes, you stay at the Washington Square Hotel in the village, room 217 under the name David Douglas.'

'Do you know where I got the name Douglas?'

'Yes, from your ex-wife, Claire Douglas.'

Salinger smiled. 'Dan, you have to admit my quick-change act has gone pretty well.'

'What do you mean your quick-change act?'

'I had a good idea once. One good, little idea. That idea turned out to be more brilliant than I'd ever imagined.'

Salinger fell silent as though he had suddenly lost interest. Or as though he believed I understood what he meant.

Maybe he was only teasing me. There was something mischievous about him, although not cruel. Was he making fun of me because he thought I was ridiculous?

I asked, 'What idea was that?'

'You know what it was,' he said. 'Everybody does.'

'I do?'

'Of course you do. Come on, Dan. I'm internationally famous for just one thing.'

'*The Catcher in the Rye?*'

'No.'

'Then what?'

'You know!'

'I do?'

'Of course you do. Want me to help you out?'

'Please.'

'The only reason I'm famous is I because I said one little word and kept on saying it. That innocent little word is no.'

'No?'

Salinger glanced at me with a worried expression on his face. 'Hey, aren't you the Dan Moller I once corresponded with? Aren't you the guy that came to the US to sell my letters?'

'Who else would I be?'

'How should I know? A clone? A double? A con artist? A Dan Moller impersonator?'

Salinger doubled up with laughter like a little kid. I could feel myself turning red, all the way to the tips of my ears.

'Take it easy, Dan. Don't punish yourself. You've been imagining me as a crazy madman who'd defend my privacy to the last drop of blood. That's what's made me rich and famous, the myth of being the only writer in the world who doesn't give interviews. It turned out to be the most profitable career move I ever made. That little word 'no' packs a greater wallop than a thousand interviews.'

'You make it sound very cold-blooded.'

'It wasn't. It was just an idea I had. I didn't feel like giving interviews, that's all it was. I just didn't feel like it. But that little idea got me more publicity and recognition than I'd ever imagined in my wildest dreams.'

'I don't believe you,' I said.

'Of course you don't. Because what would there be left to admire? An old man and a couple of books. The world's full of books.'

'Does that mean you sat down coldly and thought out a crafty long term career strategy?'

'Of course not! It was just a thought, a feeling. I realised I could simply say no. No one else did, except me. Later it turned out to be a brilliant move.'

'Whose idea was it?'

'It was more a feeling, the desire to politely refuse. It seemed completely innocent, even a bit childish. I wanted to mind my own business. Just because I've written a book about a disturbed young man doesn't mean I have to bare my personal life to the entire world, does it?'

'No.'

'If I'd hired an advertising agency to come up with ideas for marketing my work they couldn't have done a better job! Agreed?'

'Yes.'

'And I wasn't even the one that thought it up.'

'Who did?'

'My girlfriend, Claire. The one I married and had kids with.'

'What did she say?'

'She said she was fed up having journalists calling all the time, journalists knocking on the door. We were young and in love. She was married to somebody else at the time and was feeling terribly guilty towards her husband. If her husband read those interviews with me, the great, successful author, it would add insult to injury and break the man's heart, she said. He wanted to be a writer himself. So one evening when we were lying in bed at a hotel in Concorde and were pretty plastered she hit on it. Never say a word to the press!'

'And you kept that promise?'

'Yes, on the whole. Even though it hasn't been easy. All that hush-hush stuff. It would have been much easier to behave normally, just like all the other writers. But . . .'

'But?'

'But then I would never have had such a terrific career. I've made millions of dollars on that little no. I've been short listed for the Nobel prize any number of times. Why? Because of one disturbed boy called Holden Caulfied? Definitely not. Simply because of a no. And because you can make a man who never gives an interview into any myth you like, you can interpret it any way you want.'

'May I quote you on that?'

'Of course. It's the truth. But nobody believes the truth. The myth of the Greta Garbo of literature is much too potent. People don't like it when their idols are knocked down.'

'May I ask you a couple of things people are curious about?'

'Of course.'

'Do you still write?'

'Five days a week. Six hours. Like I've always done.'

'You haven't published anything in 40 years.'

'Who says so?'

'I do.'

'And you know that for a fact, do you?'

'What do you do with what you write?'

'Publish it.'

'Publish it? Where?'

'Under a pen name.'

'I don't believe it!'

'Of course you don't. But if you read very carefully you can tell which books are mine.'

'Can't you just mention one title?'

'Why not just enjoy a book or a short story in the New Yorker without worrying about who wrote it?'

'Do you write short stories for the New Yorker too? Why don't you just use your own name?'

'Because I like living in peace. I'm a man who enjoys life, Dan. I like going to the post office. I like shopping at the supermarket. I like driving and biking and taking the bus and the train. But preferably without being noticed.'

'How many books have you written under a pen name?'

'You'd have to ask my agent.'

'Dorothy Ober?'

'Yes.'

'Ha! Try getting something out of her!'

'Dotty Ober has sworn that when she dies all the letters I wrote her throughout the years will be destroyed.'

'How are your books received, the ones published under another name?'

'Fine! I've even won prizes.'

'Which you haven't accepted?'

'Which my publisher accepted on behalf of one of my aliases. Don't you think I learnt anything from Kierkegaard?'

'What time do you start work in the morning?' I asked.

He laughed. 'Oh, so we're doing one of those Paris Review interviews, are we? The writer-in-his- workshop thing. I've read them all. Faulkner's advice to kill your darlings. Hemingway's advice to stop every day before the well runs dry. And Francoise Sagan, that well-brought-up 17-year-old girl living at home with her parents one summer and writing Bonjour Tristesse in a notebook in pencil. I eat it all up!'

'Do you write by hand too?'

'OK, let's play Paris Review. I go to the office every morning just like any other office worker. I clock in at 9 and clock out at 3. I work lying on the sofa, and I write by hand. I use yellow, lined paper that I always buy at a certain shop. I use a wooden slab my son Matthew once made me for my birthday as a solid base. I have lots of rituals when I write, but it doesn't bother me if they break down because I love writing. Writing is my joy and my delight. I've never suffered from writer's block. A lot of what I write is crap but I'm good at crumpling it up and throwing it in the waste paper basket. When I've finished something by hand I type it up. I used to use a Corona because I knew that was what Hemingway used. Now I use a computer. I love my little laptop.'

'What are you working on now?'

'I've always been very fond of Hans Christian Andersen. I'm trying to write a collection of fairy tales.'

'What are they about?'

'I don't know before I begin. I just don't want them to seem like fairy tales. If Andersen were alive today he would have done it differently. Maybe I'm trying to write what Andersen would have written today. That's why I go to Denmark so much.'

'You go *where*?'

'Well, you know how much I love Kierkegaard and Karen Blixen. It's obvious in my books. I even quote them. So I had to see their country, and Andersen's.

'Where did you go to in Denmark?'

'Oh, all over. I've even been to the street where you live.'

'Holy shit, Salinger! Are you having me on?'

'Why should I be? Why shouldn't I take a trip to Europe? Why shouldn't I stroll down that tree-lined path in the King's Garden and have the thrill of seeing him at the end of it? My idol! My friend! My confidant!

Andersen. Andersen with his hand raised as if he were saying, 'Welcome to Denmark, Jerry. This is where I was born.'

'Why didn't you ring the bell when you there?'

'I saw your name downstairs in Nansensgade and at the Factory in Gothersgade, but I didn't feel right about just barging in and disturbing you.'

'*Disturbing* me!'

'I know you're busy.'

'Who told you that?'

Salinger unzipped his windbreaker. He reached into an inside pocket and took out a large envelope. The envelope was made of some kind of thick, grey paper. He handed it to me.

'Here they are,' he said.

'What are they?'

'The letters.'

'What letters?'

'Your letters.'

'*My* letters?'

He nodded. 'The letters you wrote me.'

I felt like a complete idiot. I hadn't given a thought to the letters I had written to Salinger back then. At that moment I had absolutely no recollection of anything I had ever written him.

'I really enjoyed your letters,' said Salinger.

I suddenly felt like jumping off the head of the Statue of Liberty. Salinger looked as though he understood how I felt. He patted me kindly on the shoulder and said: 'I get

191

lots of mail from admirers, but your letters were special. Also, they came at a time in my life when I was having a lot of problems and I felt like I was just a second-rate scribbler without any talent. You hailed me from the land of Kierkegaard and somehow that comforted me. He was an expert on all the schemes we human beings devise to avoid complications in our relationships. Kierkegaard is family. He's a friend. And from the very first I felt you were too. So I'm returning your letters now with thanks. Including the letters from my friend Ib. And please give his daughter Beate my very best.' I took the grey envelope and put it in my back pack. Then I quickly handed him his letters.

He took the letters, glanced at me, and nodded.

Then he was gone.

SEVENTEEN

Amanda's Tale

I didn't have to re-read the letters I had written Salinger to know what was in them, but Ib's letters were new to me. I read them at one stretch that night after Beate had fallen asleep in our double bed at the hotel.

Reading Ib's letters to Salinger was like hearing his voice, like being reunited with a member of the family. Ib had changed my life. I shudder to think how things would have turned out if I had never met him. Or not turned out. Probably the latter. His letters were written by hand. I could hear his voice. The correspondence had taken place over a period of years and the letters were in English. They always began the same: 'Dear Jerry.' All except two of Salinger's letters to Ib were typed on the same model typewriter his friend Hemingway used, as he explained.

I knew Salinger's letters by heart, and my own letters held no surprises, but when I read Ib's letters all the pieces fell into place.

The Salinger Syndrome as it stood was the result of Ib's and Salinger's combined efforts, and they had taken it as far as they could. Now Ib was dead and Salinger had certainly written his last letter to Denmark. If anyone was going to delve deeper into the theory it would have to be me.

I was on my own now, Ib Schroder and Jerry Salinger had bade me farewell and sent me on my way. I fell into a deep depression; I could feel it engulfing me. Fortunately I was completely exhausted so I fell asleep.

I opened my eyes, turned over in the bed and saw, not my wife, but Amanda. She was lying on her side and looking me straight in the eyes. She was so close that I could feel her breath in my mouth.

'Where's Beate?' I asked.

'She's been up for hours. She's visiting an old school friend who lives out in Larchmont.'

'How do you know that?'

'She left a note.'

'When did you get here?'

'Dan, I work for you. I come when you call.'

'Who gave you permission to lie here with no clothes on?'

'How do you know I'm not wearing any clothes?'

'I can feel it, I can see it.'

'You've never looked at me before, Dan.'

'Well, I'm looking at you now. I can feel you.'

'I'm a woman. You did know that, didn't you?'

'Yes, but not like that.'

'Like what?'

'Amanda, keep your hands to yourself!'

Amanda edged closer to me and whispered: 'Just keep looking at me the way you are now.'

I pushed her away. 'You're not wearing any clothes. What do you want?'

'I just want you to look at me, Dan. Look at me for the first time. We've lived together for so many years.'

I closed my eyes and kept them closed, feeling the heat emanating from Amanda's body.

She whispered: 'You knew I was in New York with you, didn't you?'

'Of course I knew.'

'So *look* at me Dan!'

'You're much younger and more beautiful than I had imagined.'

Amanda slid a hand between my legs.

'What are you doing?' I squawked.

'It's not that hard to understand.'

'Are you out of your mind?'

Amanda bent over me and started licking my ear lobe.

'Amanda?' I said, trying to make my voice sound calm. 'You're not my girlfriend. We're not man and wife.'

'No, but I could become your mistress.'

'You're way out of line. Move away please.'

'No I won't move away please. Not unless you move closer please.'

'No. I won't.'

'Look at me, Dan. For the first time, really look at me and keep on looking at me.'

She pushed aside the blanket to reveal herself lying naked beside me.

'Look at me, Dan,' she ordered.

I faced the wall and closed my eyes.

She whispered: 'Dan? Dan? Open your eyes and look at me. Do it!'

I opened my eyes and saw Amanda, all of Amanda. Amanda's body from head to foot.

She asked, 'Aren't you going to thank me?'

'What should I thank you for?'

'Don't you realize what's happening?'

'No, Amanda, but I have a feeling you're going to tell me.'

'You're seeing me for the first time.'

'I'm going to close my eyes now and you're going to get out of bed and get dressed.'

'Not until you've thanked me.'

'For what?'

'Don't you even know that?'

'OK, thanks, Amanda. I have no idea what I'm thanking you for. Or how to go about it.'

'You can thank me by going out with me and meeting some of my friends here in New York.'

'You have friends here?'

'Let's go see them. I have a right to have some fun too. I've been your traveling companion for so many years, now it's my turn to be the main character for a while.'

Amanda pulled off the rest of the blanket and started tugging at my pyjamas. I resisted. She used force. I defended myself as well as I could. Although I tried to fight her off, a moment later I was naked.

'Goddammit , Dan, you're not 7 years old anymore!

Grow up. You have a body. Your depression is part of that body.'

'So?'

'Use your body, man. Give yourself over to it.'

'I don't believe what I'm hearing. Are you suggesting we have sex?'

'Why not?'

'That would be incest or masturbation or some other kind of perversion. You don't have sex with your *depression*!'

'Why not?'

'Amanda, you've got a sick mind. A sick mind in a sick body.'

'You knew that all along, you hypocrite.'

'Yes, but I didn't know you were so beautiful.'

'So tell me I'm beautiful and you want me.'

'If I do, will you promise to leave me alone?'

'Yes, I promise.'

'Amanda, you're beautiful and I really want to have sex with you.'

'Dan, you're beginning to have your own eyes. It only took 45 years. Congratulations!'

'I'm halfway through life.'

'Are you counting on reaching 90?'

'Yes.'

'Well, you won't unless you stay on my good side.'

'I know.'

She said: 'That's why I think I have the right to have some fun too.'

'What did you have in mind?'

'Come with me, you'll see.'

Amanda got out of bed. She stood there naked on the floor.

She opened the closet and started going through Beate's things. 'Your wife has good taste in clothes.'

'Does Beate know you're here?'

Amanda put on a pair of black panties and smiled. 'Not unless you told her.'

'I didn't.'

'Don't you think it's about time?'

'I'll have to lie and say you're old and ugly.'

Amanda was putting on Beate's bra. 'Do you think I'm old and ugly?'

'Amanda, you're flirting with me. It's embarrassing. Did Nora put you up to this?'

'Hey, loosen up. I'm a woman, get that through your head.'

'Did you always look like this?'

'Dan, your questions are getting stupider and stupider.'

She pulled a striped dress down over her head.

I got out of bed and turned my back to her.

She chuckled. 'I know all about you, kid. You can't hide anything from me. Hurry up and get dressed so we can go out.'

'Where are we going?'

'On an adventure. Amanda's adventure.'

'Where does Amanda's adventure lead ?'

'Where do you think?'

'I don't think anything.'

'You know what my name means, don't you?

'Yes.'

'Say it then.'

'Why?'

'Because that's where my adventure leads.'

'Amanda means she that shall be loved.'

'Exactly.'

'Exactly what?'

'Dan, pull yourself together intelligence-wise, otherwise it'll just get too boring.'

'Who's supposed to love you?' I asked.

'Who do you think? *You* are, Dan.'

'Why should I? You can't make somebody love you by force.'

'Dan, I find it difficult to believe you're as stupid as you sound.'

'What's so stupid about me?'

'You think all I am is your enemy. I'm not. I'm your friend, too. I've given you everything!'

'All you've given me is depression.'

'You're *nothing* without me, Dan. Face it. Do you really think Boris, Nora and Puk would have anything to do with you without me? Without me you would never have met Ib, you would never have met Salinger, and you wouldn't have Beate.'

She hurled herself at me through the air, knocking me over backwards onto the bed. She pinned me down and lay on top of me, a triumphant smile on her face.

All I could do was smile back.

'OK, Amanda. You win. Tell me what to do and I'll do it.'

'Simple. I've faithfully accompanied you on all your journeys. It's time you paid me back.'

'How.'

'Take a journey with me. Amanda's journey.'

We left the room and went downstairs. There was such a crowd on Broome Street it was impossible to take a single step. It took a while to realise they were all journalists and photographers. Suddenly I realized that it was me they had all come to see; they wanted to interview, film and photograph me, Dan T. Moller. I just managed to catch a glimpse of Amanda nodding at me when I was besieged on all sides with questions and flashes.

'Is it true you've discovered a cure for depression?'

'No, it isn't true.'

'What's all this about the Salinger Syndrome then?'

'The Salinger Syndrome is just one way of describing one specific form of depression.'

'Was it invented by the American writer J.D. Salinger?'

'Yes, by him, my father-in-law and myself, based on work by the Danish philosopher Soren Kierkegaard in 1840.'

'Is it true you've discovered a drug for that type of depression?'

'Not a drug. A treatment.'

'A treatment called the Kierkegaard Cure?'

'Yes.'

'Is it true that hundreds of people suffering from that type of depression here in New York have been trying to contact you?'

'I hope not. I want to be an anonymous tourist in New York.'

'How much do you charge for a treatment?'

'I don't know yet.'

'How does it feel to be suddenly famous?'

'It's just happened so I don't know.'

'Is it true that you've come to New York to treat Andy Warhol for depression?'

'Does Andy Warhol suffer from depression?'

A big black limousine was inching its way through the crowd.

It came to a halt in front of where Amanda and I were standing. I immediately recognised the man who got out, Andy Warhol, Mr. Pop himself, as he was called: the inventor of pop art, artist, movie director, cultural icon. He had once paid a brief visit to Denmark. His Danish hosts were acquaintances of Puk and Nora. Warhol knew that our Factory in Gothersgade had been modeled on his own Factory in New York. Warhol visited our factory. It was the only time in the entire history of the Factory that we received a visit. Warhol showed up with a small entourage consisting of Margit and Erik Brandt, Ellen and Jorgen Norgaard and Niels Barfoed. Warhol had already spoken with Puk whom he had met several times in New York. Warhol was the only person I had ever seen Puk admire unconditionally and fanatically. Warhol had a Danish dealer called Hansen, who sold Warhol's work in Denmark. Hansen was a passionate Kierkegaard aficionado. He got the idea that someone should write a play about Soren Kierkegaard and approached a number of Danish authors about it. He put up a fair amount of money, regardless of the result. In Hansen's opinion Warhol was a modern-day Kierkegaard. I was present at a discussion of the subject between Hansen and Puk. It took place one late afternoon on the pedestrian crossing on the corner of Norre Voldgade and Gothersgade at rush hour.

'Pure nonsense,' said Puk to Hansen when he compared Warhol to Kierkegaard.

'Why is it nonsense?' Hansen wanted to know.

Puk replied: 'Warhol is a sphinx without a secret, a mirror. Behind it he's a vacuum.'

'Precisely,' said Hansen. 'So was Kierkegaard. Kierkegaard is the greatest pop philosopher in history.'

'Kierkegaard is a religious philosopher,' countered Puk.

'So is Warhol. He goes to mass every morning. He's deeply religious.'

'Hansen, for Christ's sake! Warhol takes pride in never reading a book. Kierkegaard was an intellectual, he attended Hegel's lectures in Berlin.'

'Come on, Puk. Andy Warhol has read Kierkegaard more carefully than you have. Warhol and Georg Brandes agree that Kierkegaard was the greatest psychologist before Freud, that his studies of the nature of depression were the best ever.'

Hansen and Puk were now standing in front of the Rosenborg castle barracks. They were getting in the way of passing pedestrians, but were so involved in their discussion that they ignored the angry comments.

They were yelling so loud they seemed to be fighting. Hansen was enjoying it. So was Puk.

Hansen shouted: 'Warhol's theories on monotony are straight out of Kierkegaard. Warhol's theories on the hidden God are more Kierkegaard than Kierkegaard.'

'Hansen, you've got rich marketing Warhol in Denmark, but you don't know a thing about Kierkegaard.'

'Listen, Puk, I've read your essays on boredom and stupidity so carefully I know them forwards and backwards.'

'What's *that* supposed to prove?'

'It proves you stole half of it from Kierkegaard and the other half from Warhol.'

That was the first time I'd ever seen Puk at a loss for words.

When she finally found her tongue her response rang out over Rosenborg castle courtyard and the King's Gardens.

'Hansen. It is my considered opinion that not only are you right, you are 100%, unconditionally right, to which fact I would gladly testify on a written document duly certified by a notary public, in duplicate should you so desire. Immediately!'

That was the end of that discussion and the beginning of Puk's and Hansen's friendship. On Hansen's next trip to New York to see Andy Warhol he took Puk along.

Puk told the rest of us at the Factory that she had been present when Warhol painted a portrait of Kierkegaard. Only two other people apart from Warhol himself had seen the painting: Hansen and Puk. Warhol had laid careful plans for what was to be done with his work and his other personal effects when he died. He had built a hundred large containers he called time capsules. On every container he had written a year. After his death, once a year, a time capsule was to be opened. The Kierkegaard container was to be opened on May 5th, 2013, the date of the two hundredth anniversary of Kierkegaard's birth.

The connection between the New York Factory and the Copenhagen Factory was so obvious that it came as no surprise to either Amanda or me to see Andy Warhol emerge from the crowd on Broome Street.

I had met Warhol once and shaken his hand. We had never exchanged more than a hello and goodbye. Just like everybody else at the Factory Warhol was much more interested in Amanda than in me. So he greeted Amanda first.

I was standing so close to them I heard every word they said.

'Amanda, baby. So nice to see you,' said Warhol squeezing in among the photographers and journalists.

'Hi, Andy. Thanks.'

'Everything ok?'

'Yes, I'm fine, Andy.'

'That's wonderful, I'm so glad.'

'So nice of you to come.'

'Does he know?'

'He doesn't know it's your plan.'

'Will he do it?'

'Sure he will.'

'Have you told him about it?'

'Only a little bit.'

'You want me to tell him?'

'Yes, Andy.'

'OK, Amanda, I love you.'

'I love you too, Andy.'

I was busy answering questions on the Salinger Syndrome when Andy elbowed his way over to me and breathed in my ear: 'Pssst, Danny.'

'Hi there, Andy.'

'You understand what's happening here, don't you?'

'I think so.'

'You're in my world, Danny, in Andy Warhol's wonderful, magic world.'

'Great.'

'Danny, when I'm dead I'll be remembered for just one thing.'

'I guess so.'

'Tell me, Danny.'

'No, I want to get it from you Andy. From the mouth of the sphinx.'

'Ok. Here goes. This is Andy Warhol on Broome Street talking to Danny T. from Denmark. In the future everybody will be famous for 15 minutes. Danny's fifteen minutes started a couple of minutes ago.'

'So these are my fifteen minutes of fame? I'm famous now?'

'You got it, baby.'

'Thank you, Andy.'

'Enjoy, Danny.'

Everyone around us was asking the same question. Did I have a cure for depression? How could they get an appointment? How much did I charge for a TV interview? How could they reach me?

Andy Warhol ushered us into the back seat of his car. Before he got in himself, he turned around and proclaimed to the journalists at large: 'This is a work of art. The whole word is a work of art. In future everyone will be happy.'

Amanda was squeezed between Warhol and me in the back seat and the limousine began to crawl through the crowd. Everyone was calling to us outside the window. It was always the same story. Either they were suffering from depression themselves, or they knew someone who was. How and when could they get more information?

Andy Warhol said, 'I've arranged a little trip for you. A trip that takes 11 minutes and has four stops. I've got four depressed colleagues who've begged me to let them meet you both.' The car drove into Chinatown and stopped in front of a dilapidated building.

Warhol pointed to the third floor.

'My fortune teller lives up there. I've used him for years. He's never wrong. His specialty is depressed artists. He was the one who advised me to become a machine. He says I'll be dead within the year.'

Andy held me by one hand and Amanda by the other. 'This is Andy Warhol, and this is the first stop on the journey. When I die, make sure I don't sizzle away for years in Purgatory like a barbecued hotdog on a flame, but let me go straight to the land of the dead.'

'How?' I asked.

'Use the syndrome and the cure,' was his reply.

I did as Warhol asked. It wasn't hard. I had spent my whole life studying it. What was Andy's post office like?

I told him: 'You have millions of admirers, Andy. They'll hold you over the fire forever, they'll never let you go. Your greatest admirer lives in Copenhagen, Puk Bonnesen. When you die I promise Puk will let you go. She'll allow you to disappear and pass over into the land of the dead.'

Amanda asked: 'How do you die, Andy? Does another admirer of yours stab you with a knife or shoot you because you have too much power over her?'

'No, this time I die of kidney failure. My kidneys cease functioning because of all the drugs I've been taking for years.'

Warhol instructed his chauffeur to drive on. We drove north to 85th Street. A small figure was standing on the sidewalk in front of a white brick apartment building waiting for us. He was wearing dark glasses and a soft grey hat. It was Woody Allen, the movie director, comedian, actor, author, the world's most famous professional depressive neurotic. Woody got into the front seat and turned to face us.

Amanda glanced at Andy and Woody in turn, and asked: 'Same story? Woody doesn't want to burn in Purgatory either?'

Woody piped, 'No, no, I'm just a garden variety depressive with great connections. Salinger and my friend Andy here got me an in with you guys. I suffer from anhedonia, I'm incapable of enjoyment. I'm the greatest admirer of Soren Kierkegaard in town, so can his cure help me?'

Amanda and I whispered to each other in Danish. What was Woody's post office like? How did he get attention, friendship, love?

Amanda and I agreed on what to advise Woody: 'First, we'll put you on a diet. Only a small number of jokes, gags and punchlines a day. You've got to bring down your poodle-begging-for-attention levels to moderate, no more than once or twice a day maximum. Come back in a month and let's see how your post office is doing then.'

Woody Allen didn't look too happy. He got out of the car and we drove on. As we approached Central Park it suddenly went from being virtually empty to overflowing with people. What appeared to be at least a million people were pursuing one lone figure running as fast as he could.

Andy Warhol got out of the car and held the door open for Elvis Presley who jumped into the back seat and sat on Amanda's lap. Andy Warhol sat on the front seat next to the driver, and told him to drive faster before we were swallowed up by the sea of people.

Elvis looked at me . 'Hi Dan.'

'Hi Elvis.'

'Do you know why I'm here?'

'You died, what is it, 12 years ago? 11? 10? Yes, 10. Now you're stuck in Purgatory and can't get out, is that it?'

'Yup.'

'Elvis, do you know how to pass over into the land of the dead.?' 'Yup, sure do, and so do you, Dan.'

Elvis knew Amanda. Elvis had suffered from depression for many years when he died of a heart attack in his home Graceland, in Memphis in 1977. The cause of death was too many pills. He was overweight, depressed, and was on all kinds of medication.

Elvis asked. 'Should we do it, Dan?'

I nodded. Elvis had been with me since 1956. I had been rowing in Hellerup Harbor when Buster Bach, the coxswain, started bawling out *Tutti Frutti*.

'What's that?' I'd asked.

'Oh, this singer that was always on the radio when I was in America.'

'What's his name?'

'Elvis Presley.'

'Is he black?'

'No, but he sings like he was.'

'Do you have any of his records?'

'Seven.'

'Can I borrow them?'

'Only if you promise to give up rowing.'

'Why?'

'You're always out of sync. I'm sorry to tell you this, but everybody hates being in your boat.'

I borrowed seven Elvis Presley 45 rpm records in return for promising to give up rowing. Elvis entered my life and stayed there. He sang to me directly from Memphis, Tennessee. One evening when I was lying in bed with Beate in the commune in Studiestræde there was a knock on the door. Two of the others, Torben and Pia, wanted to make a date for the next day. Just before they left, Pia said, 'Oh, by the way, have you heard the news? Elvis Presley is dead.'

I burst into tears. In terms of music I've been crying ever since. That's what Elvis pointed out to me in the car driving through Central Park. Ten years later he was dead.

'Dan, you're keeping me a prisoner in Purgatory as long as you cry. Of all my millions of fans you're the one that makes the difference. Dry your tears and set me free so I can pass over into the land of the dead.'

I dried my musical tears. He was dead but I still had his music, I consoled myself. No more childish dreams; the King would not return.

Amanda opened her window and Elvis floated out. He beamed down at us on his way up. He was becoming fainter. Before he was gone completely he called down to us, 'So long, my friends. We'll meet again in the land of the dead.'

The car drove out of Central Park at a rapid clip. Everywhere there were Elvis fans looking up into the sky where he had disappeared.

A voice boomed out: 'Elvis has departed this earth. God save Elvis. There is no cause for alarm. Elvis has finally arrived where he wishes to be. Elvis has departed this earth.'

The car turned south again and stopped in front of the Empire State Building. Long lines of people were waiting at the entrance to tell me about their depression, their own depression or their friends' or families'. Guards were called to protect Amanda, Warhol and me. We were taken by elevator to the observation deck from where we could survey all of New York.

We circled the viewing area until we reached what we had come to see. Far above us there was a figure suspended in the air. Squinting, we strained to see who it was. It was Ernest Hemingway, author, Nobel Prize winner, deceased 26 years ago.

He called down to us. 'Help me. I've been stuck in Purgatory for an eternity. Help me cross over into the land of the dead.'

Hemingway had committed suicide in 1961. He had shot himself in the head with a shotgun. His father had committed suicide the same way. After his father had shot himself Hemingway's mother had sent him the weapon his father had used to kill himself.

I called up to Hemingway: 'What can I do to get you out?'

He called back: 'Make that guy who has me by the balls let go of me. So long as he's hanging onto them I can't move on.'

'Who is it?'

'Your pal, Boris Schauman.'

Andy Warhol handed me a pair of binoculars so I could make out what was going on up there.

Underneath Hemingway, half hidden by a cloud, hung Boris. He was trying to use Hemingway's balls as a lever.

'Boris!' I called to him. 'It's me, Dan. Let the man go for God's sake so he can get out of Purgatory.'

Boris didn't answer; he was too busy hanging on.

Hemingway shouted: 'Dan, do something. Call off your friend. I've been waiting for you for so many years.'

Hemingway was right, of course. I was the only one who knew how to make Boris loosen his grip.

I summoned all the members of the Danish Academy to New York from Rungstedlund. Forming a squadron they took off from the top of the Empire State Building in two ranks, women in one rank, men in the other, aiming straight at their respective targets. The female members of the academy grabbed hold of one of Boris' testicles, the men the other. The weight of the entire Danish Academy was so overwhelming that Boris was forced to loosen his grip on Hemingway's balls. As the Danes drifted off over the Hudson, Hemingway floated upwards and disappeared. He nodded, smiled and disappeared into the land of the dead.

Andy Warhol checked his watch. 'Three minutes to go before your fifteen minutes of fame are up, Dan. You have one last meeting.'

Darkness had fallen on New York. Below us the city lights were coming on.

Andy Warhol whispered: 'Who's the most famous person in town?'

Somewhere up in the sky above us someone called to us. 'Amanda? Dan? Can you hear me? Up here!'

We looked up. Hovering in the night sky above Manhattan was Marilyn Monroe. She was wearing a white dress. A breeze was tugging at the bottom of her dress, lifting it so you could see the edge of her panties.

She waved to us. 'Amanda? Dan? Can you see me?'

'Yes.'

'Help me. Get me out of jail.'

'What jail?' called Amanda.

Marilyn pointed to her dress that had now blown up even higher, exposing her rear end. 'The jail of being a sex queen. I'm the biggest inflatable jerk-off doll in the world. More men jerk off on me than anyone else in the whole world. Dan, I beg you. I'm not just tits and ass. I've met your Karen Blixen. She knows I'm spirit and intellect too. Give me back my body. Release me!'

'But how?' we called.

A faint whisper drifted up to us from all the houses and streets. A woman's voice was sighing, 'Dan and Amanda, Amanda and Dan, help me, set me free.'

It was the voice of a million small faces down below. Faces on posters, on coffee mugs and T shirts, on can openers, jewelry, on any marketable commodity. It was the face of Marilyn Monroe who had committed suicide after a long depression in 1962. She killed herself by taking too many pills.

A million voices down below whispered to us: 'Help me! Help me get out of purgatory.'

Help came swiftly this time. Back in Copenhagen Nora was walking down Gothersgade when she got the message. Nora was the obvious candidate for this job. She crossed the street and entered the Botanical Gardens. She squatted on the grass. Cupping her hands in front of her face, she exhaled gently in puffs and gusts, murmuring: 'Marilyn, Marilyn, Marilyn.'

Her words wafted over Copenhagen, drifted west over Denmark and continued across the North Sea, becoming a hurricane as they crossed the Atlantic. Hurricane warnings were issued for the greater New York area and Hurricane Marilyn slammed into the city. The hurricane tore into the millions of pictures of Marilyn Monroe on posters, billboards and objects. The pictures whirled together forming an image that filled the sky above New York. Marilyn waved goodbye. In the city below not one single image of her was left. She was out of Purgatory now and a moment later passed over into the land of the dead.

At that moment my fifteen minutes of fame were up. Amanda, Warhol and I were free to take the elevator down to the street without being noticed.

Amanda took my hand as we walked down the street.

Andy took leave of us at Union Square. 'My fortune teller informs me I'll be dead in a few months. When I am, I'd like to ask you a favor, Dan.'

'Of course.'

'Put me in a little corner of the Salinger Syndrome. Include a sub-section on the Warhol cure. Love your depression. That's my advice, Warhol's advice: Love Amanda. She's given you everything. Give her what we all need, kindness, attention, love.

Andy raised his hand in farewell and disappeared into the crowd.

At that very moment, standing there in Union Square, looking after Andy Warhol, it happened, what I had prayed for my whole life. I got my own eyes. It was a calm, peaceful experience. The eyes I was seeing with were now my own, and the voice I spoke with when I opened my mouth was my own too.

'Amanda, I love you.'

'I know,' she said and put her arm around my neck and kissed me.

'How long have you known, Amanda?'

'None of your business,' she said and kissed me again.

EIGHTEEN

All Adventures Come to an End

I'm the only one at the Factory with fixed working hours. I'm always at work on the stroke of 8 and leave at precisely 4.15 p.m.

We never arrive at the factory at the same time in the morning. Only once in the history of the Factory did we all meet in the morning on the sidewalk in front of the Factory. It was late January 2010. Turning the corner from Oster Farimagsgade I saw a sight I'd never seen before: Puk, Boris and Nora were standing on the sidewalk in front of the door to the Factory.

My first thought was that the door was stuck, the lock was broken. When I reached them Nora said quietly, 'Salinger is dead.'

'Where did you hear that?' I asked evenly.

Puk said, 'It was on the Internet last night. I've been up all night working.'

Boris pointed out, 'He was 91.'

My first thought was of a dead plant, the plant Salinger had stolen from Freud's garden in London was dead now; it had withered and Salinger died the next day.

My eyes filled with tears and a moment later tears were running down my cheeks.

Nora had a handkerchief ready. She smiled at me. 'I'm glad you're crying Dan. You were fond of Salinger and he deserves your tears.'

I dried my eyes. The other three looked at each other to see which of them going to tell me what they had agreed. The lot fell on Boris. 'The rest of us talked last night. It turns out we all have pretty much the same reaction to Salinger's death and it seems none of us knows why.'

He fell silent and looked at Puk and Nora.

It was Nora's turn: 'We decided once many years ago that we wanted the factory to last our whole lives. So we agreed never to rock the boat by seeing each other privately and risk draining all the energy out of our friendship.'

Puk took over. 'That was my idea, back then. Now I have another idea. I suggest we become friends, personal friends. If you want to be friends with me, that is, and with the others?'

I replied, 'Salinger would have understood perfectly.'

We celebrated the start of our new friendship by not going to work that day. We walked down Gothersgade, turned right into Kronprinsessegade and sat down in Café Sommersko.

We stayed there over coffee until lunchtime. After lunch we stayed on until we'd got hold of our families. And there, along with our husbands and wives and children and grandchildren and a dog concealed in a bag we all had dinner together for the first time.

Boris' oldest son Carl raised his glass: 'To Salinger', he said.

The rest of us joined in, repeating in unison: 'To Salinger.'

I turned and looked straight into Beate's eyes.

And then for the first time in I thought of Ulla Ladegaard, my fairy tale therapist. I hadn't thought of her since I had made her a promise all those years ago. I'm thinking of you now, Ulla, when you said love is what moves the sun and the stars.